MW01613033

All other produce names and services identified throughout this book are trademarks or registered trademarks of their respective companies. They are used throughout this book in editorial fashion only and for the benefit of such companies. No such uses, or the use of any trade name, is intended to convey endorsement or other affiliation with the book.

The information and material contained in this book is true and complete to the best of our knowledge and is provided "as is," without warranty of any kind, express or implied, including without limitation any warranty concerning the accuracy, adequacy, or completeness of such information or material or the results to be obtained from using such information or material neither Morris Publishing, Heartland Publishing or the author shall be responsible for any claims attributable to errors, omissions, or other inaccuracies in the information or material contained in this book, and in no event shall Morris Publishing, Heartland Publishing or the author be liable for direct, indirect, special incidental, or consequential damages arising out of the use of such information or material.

Published by Heartland Publishing
P.O. Box 1374
Huron, South Dakota 57350
Electronic mail address: unisonia@usa.net

Editor: Margaret Moxon - Cheryl Krutzfeldt - Ellen Storm

Cover Art and Design: Collin Loesch - Tom Sondreal - Ivan Loesch

Wordprocessing: Elaine Loesch - Mary Anne Keefe - Fawn Glanzer - Ellen Storm

Design and Composition: Mary Anne Keefe - Ivan Loesch

Book Production: Morris Publishing - Kearney, NE

Printed and manufactured in the United States of America on recycled Acid-free paper
10 9 8 7 6 5 4 3 2 1

Loesch, Ivan L. 1936
Unisonia: a Doable Global Village/Ivan L. Loesch

Library of Congress
Catalog Card Number: 99-94368
ISBN: 0-7392-0179-4

Unisonia® is a service mark of Ivan L. Loesch

Printed in the USA by

MORRIS PUBLISHING

3212 East Highway 30 • Kearney, NE 68847 • 1-800-650-7888

# UNISONIA

------------------------------------

## IVAN L. LOESCH

# PUBLISHER

Heartland Publishing

Successful Solutions you can use
in your Community

# DEDICATION

I have chosen to dedicate this book to my wife, Elaine
who has so patiently updated the many edits of the manuscript,
and to our children, Curt, Lynn (Tom Nelson),and Collin, grandchildren,
Erik and Kayla Nelson, and to all those actively seeking a mutually
self-sustaining, better world.

## *TAKING RISKS IS PART OF LIFE*

*To laugh is to Risk appearing the fool.*
*To weep is to Risk appearing sentimental.*
*To reach for another is to Risk involvement.*
*To expose your ideas, your dreams before a crowd,*
*is to Risk their loss.*
*To love is to Risk not being loved in return.*
*To live is to Risk dying.*
*But Risks must be taken,*
*because the greatest hazard in life is to Risk nothing.*
*They may avoid suffering and sorrow,*
*but they cannot learn, feel change, grow, love, live.*
*Chained by their attitudes, they are slaves;*
*they have forfeited their freedom.*
*Only a person who Risks is free.*

*Author Unknown*

*A happy person is not a person in a certain set of circumstances, but*
*rather a person with a certain set of attitudes.*

# ACKNOWLEDGEMENTS

In writing this book, our community of Unisonian friends has expanded beyond anything I could have imagined. Proper thanks listing each and every one by name will never be possible to all those who have helped in so many ways in making this book a reality.

Numerous people have given guidance and clarification. They have added resource material and offered positive critiques as well as very important moral support.

Many of those who were so helpful are as follows:

Rev. Conrad and Vavie Aamodt, Donna and Tom Bartholow, Jen Bixby, Donald Cook, James Ciassio, Former Governor Frank Farrar, Janice Farrar, Joanne Groves, William Haley, Patrick Haley, Chris Hedlund, Edward Hogan, MaryEllen Johnson, Dave Keefe, Tom Killian, Kevin Kleinjan, Tom Leathers, John Luther, Bryan Majares, Dennis and Bertha Moriarity, Crystal Pugsley, Cary and Karen Radowitz, Professor Gretchen Rich, Rollyn Samp, Professor/Coach Linda Olson Sandness, Professor James Satterly, Judy Schmitt, Ryan Schmitt, Brenda Seifert, Fred Silbernagel, Tom Sorrenson, Professor Rus Stubbles, Robert Taylor, Phil Thomas, Former Governor Harvey and Ann Wollman , James Zurbrigen, Professor Dennis Healy and his South Dakota State University Landscape Architecture Class - Mike Bruner, Brian Butler, Tony Fratzke, Cary Goering, Justin Van Hall, Stu Hansen, Harvey Hubbard, Chad Jensen, Sarah Jensen, Brent Kemnitz, Kyle Korver, Chad Lamer, Cory Liepold, Keith Louwagie, Mark Van Meteren, Ryan Miller, Curtis Mulder, Ron Peterson, Mat Reker, Brad Rippentrop, Matt Stensland, Brent Venenga, Tricia Wheeler, Marilyn Hofer and her communications class, Mitchel Gaffer and his speaking and debate class.

# Attitude

"The longer I live, the more I realize the impact of attitude on life. Attitude, to me, is more important than facts. It is more important than the past, than education, than money, than circumstances, than failures, than successes, than what other people think or say or do. It is more important than appearance, giftedness, or skill. It will make or break a company...a church...a home. The remarkable thing is we have a choice every day regarding the attitude we will embrace for that day. We cannot change our past...we cannot change the fact that people will act in a certain way. We cannot change the inevitable. The only thing we can do is play on the one string we have, and that is our attitude...I am convinced that life is 10% what happens to me and 90% how I react to it. And so it is with you ~ we are in charge of our Attitudes."

~ *Charles Swindoll*

# UNISONIA

What OTHERS are saying:

MARTIN BUSCH - dramatic reader South Dakota Public Radio
"Ivan Loesch not only describes his innovative and comprehensive, pre-planned community for now and the future; he also does it in a simple, easy-to-read style for all ages. The page format is interesting with comfortable open spaces along with many explanatory illustrations. It invites one to read it."


WILLIAM M. PFAUTZ - Minister
"I, personally, found *Unisonia* easy to read with a good flow of information. Your idea of Unisonia with the Uni-Citi, Uni-Quad, and Uni-Parks concept is intriguing and appears to have many practical aspects that are important."

## UNI-CITI PROTOTYPE PLAN
### Ivan L. Loesch, Copyright 1999
### Creator-Designer

The Uni-Citi plan, its design, detail and invention is the property of Ivan L. Loesch, and shall not be copied in any manner without the consent of Ivan L. Loesch.

Ivan L. Loesch is not obligated to use ideas presented at brain-storming sessions, nor is he obligated to remunerate participants for ideas which may be spoken or otherwise presented.

The information in this book is intended to spark your imagination and encourage you in your belief that practical community change toward improvement of the *total person* within the *total community* is not only possible but doable as well.

Dream Your Life ~ Achieve it in UNISONIA. Be a modern day Empire Builder. Bring excitement back into your life.

# UNISONIA

U ni son i a  (u'no so'ni o) n.    1. harmonious combination or union
of people, processes and material into systematic solutions to human
needs in  a planned community.   2. a Mutual Enterprise System which
may include a creative, satisfying, environmentally, conservation and
human friendly way of life.


*Unisonia - a place where people understand their obligation and
responsibility to their neighbors and themselves with use of their
longterm commitment to an experimental prototype exercise in human
environments.*

~ Ivan L. Loesch


*Make no little plans,
they have no magic to stir (people's) blood.*
~ *Daniel Hudson Burnham*

# CONTENTS

## UNISONIA
### By Ivan L. Loesch

# PART III-COMMUNICATIONS AND COMPUTERIZATION 139

# UNISONIA

# UNISONIA

## A UNISONIA INTRODUCTION
### PLENTY, HAPPINESS AND PEACE:
### In Search for a Utopia

by
David W. Conlin, Ph.D.

## LOESCHS' UNISONIA,
## A MORE HUMANE ENVIRONMENT

Ivan Loesch is presenting a basic alternative in achieving a more humane environment through UNISONIA. Loesch believes that much can be done to redirect human energy toward a more abundant life for the inhabitants of this earth. Even though the so-called utopia is so illusive, UNISONIA will point out many successfully achieved programs which have improved the human lot in many places. Combining them into a system cannot help but improve the human condition to a great degree.

In our mass production, over consumption, immediate gratification, and self-interest oriented society in the United States today, we find a highly complex, advanced technological economic system based on free enterprise doing its very best to usher in a modern day utopia. Despite our individual and collective diligence to achieve this desirable goal, characterized by the beneficent ideals of peace, happiness, and plenty for some mystifying reason, still remain beyond our realization.

Because of our lack of success in reaching this ideal goal, we should in retrospect pause and take a moment to ponder what we have accomplished in striving toward this end and how close we are in attaining it today. Perhaps through an endemic analysis of the extreme emphasis placed upon the third characteristic of our utopia - "plenty" - can we find answers to this question and as to why the other two characteristics - peace and happiness - still remain elusive. In so doing, perhaps we can gain an enlightened insight into new alternative recommendations and directions necessary to achieve this universal goal in the near or distant future.

## Capitalism - The Horn of Plenty

Adam Smith, the 18th century advocate of self-interest and laissez-faire and acclaimed original modern day proponent of capitalism, based his well-intended justification for private enterprise upon the following principle: Public interest is best served by selfish individuals. He believed that by pursuing one's own self interest, man will frequently promote the overall interest of society.

At first glance, this is certainly an intriguing and attractive proposal simply because it is based upon the practical individual expression of free agency, an opportunity that all people desire to exercise. As a result of his enticing economic theory as well as our country's unique political and geographical circumstances for its application, capitalism was adopted and has been successfully practiced over the last several centuries as evidenced by our abundant material wealth.

Milton Friedman, the latest and probably the foremost economist, also concurs and supports the Adam Smith theory by stressing the point which states that the free market system allows for both individual freedom and social welfare. Capitalism is successful in satisfying both these areas that are so important to both men and women individually and society collectively. The only alternative that he believes is feasible but unacceptable is central direction with its inherent power of coercion which together will extinguish individual freedom that historically we so very much cherished. He believes, therefore, that the absence of central coercion is essential to the functioning of a free democratic market system. Under capitalism, democracy is insured because the consumer is allowed to decide what is produced by voting with his dollars. Inherent profit incentive will insure that what each individual desires will be produced.

*Reasonable profit is necessary and appropriate for those exerting mental and physical energy. Equal pay for equal work is also appropriate. Greed is not.*

*~ Ivan L. Loesch*

As good as the system of capitalism is meant to be, there are significant hazards and shortcomings I believe Smith never anticipated and Friedman continues to overlook. They are as follows:

1. The desire for materialistic greed is often insatiable. Original proponents of capitalism never did conceive that man's desire for material things can or would become unlimited. Neither did they conceive of new and present means of mass media such as the TV and radio that can bombard the senses incessantly and subliminally to intensify the desire for more things while simultaneously reducing a sense of

satisfaction for what is already possessed. The full scope of the reign and effects of materialism has and continues to be not well understood as to the adverse ramifications it poses for man and society and his environment.

2. The concept of bigness as manifested in centralization and stimulated by the incentive of increased profit margins has often overstepped its usefulness when it can

*"What some people mistake for the high cost of living is really the cost of living high."*

~ **Doug Larson**

dominate and manipulate economics and politics worldwide. Mass and rapid communication, transportation, technology, and specialization have all made this possible, even much more so today than several decades ago.

3. Third world countries have simply become personal serfdoms for International Corporations.

4. Capitalist proponents have based their conception and the feasibility of free enterprise on past altruistic, conservative ideas and values which today have degenerated or are no longer practiced, thus reducing and restricting free enterprise. Values such as charity, responsibility, discipline, and hard work have been superseded or replaced by the need for acceptance, prestige, status, power and greed, only which money is thought to provide. Get rich quick with as little effort as possible through investment speculation has undermined the puritan work ethic and alienated each individual from his fellow man.

Despite the foregoing shortcomings and criticisms of capitalism -- a free market system characterized by greed, envy and over-consumption as the dominating motive many people within the system as well as its proponents perhaps can't be entirely blamed for their materialistic ideological behavior. After all, everyone wants some share of the good life, however that may be defined. Nevertheless, when someone attempts to achieve prosperity at the expense of others, that person as with anyone else, will become victimized and exploited on the cyclic road to peace, prosperity and plenty.

The foregoing statement of existing socio-economics deficiencies is not an indictment that capitalism is an archaic principle that is no longer useful. The intent however is only to reiterate that capitalism can pose myriads of obstacles in the path to peace and happiness, and therefore, perhaps a modification of its underlying assumptions and foundations can lead us to alternative economic systems that are less debilitating to people's security and spirit.

> *We are what we have learned from the past, what we experience today, and what we dream for tomorrow.*
>
> ~ **Ivan L. Loesch**

### Materialism - The Bottomless Well
The essence of materialism is not essential to provide the basic requirements of life: food, shelter, and clothing for human physical well-being. Materialism should not exist for the productive use of all humanity. History has repeatedly demonstrated that once our basic requirements are satisfied through the diligence, organization, and cooperation of people working together, people will inevitably raise their expectations of what new material things they must have to be happy and content.

As a result of our capacity to produce more, the philosophy of -- get all you can because the more you have the better off you will be -- has taken precedence over any past or present enlightened inner beliefs of what peace and happiness really are or thought to be.

Because self-centeredness is the basis of capitalism-materialism, man's intrinsic mental desire for status, prestige, success, and therefore security and acceptance can best be fulfilled readily by what he obtains and by what he consumes. With everyone working for their own self interest, the tenet of capitalism thus creates a vicious spiral of eternal desire and need for more and more goods -- greater wealth. The criterion for success then is measured by one's position, power, wealth, not by parameters such as peace, happiness, or service to mankind. Consequently, materialism increases as the emphasis on humanistic concerns and services decreases, thus posing a myriad of social - spiritual problems for many people within the system.

**Multinational Abuse from a Third World Perspective**

Because size and centralized power are important and unique facets characteristic of large corporations, nations less developed, but rich in natural resources have become victimized socially, economically, and politically by multinational exploitation. Socially, for example, third world countries have been encouraged to promote birth control with the hope that a stable indigenous population will insure an ample supply of desirable resources for the developed nations. Economically, the United States via corporations has invested several billion dollars in these less developed countries, it has during this period of time extracted approximately the same amount. Our country has used its financial and military muscle to support dictatorships friendly toward our companies' goals. Environmentally we have diligently and inexpensively extracted natural resources with little regard to environmental abuses. In retrospect, it is rather sad what one developed country can conceivably do to another less developed countries simply because its needs for plenty, thought to be prerequisite to a utopian state, has become insatiable.

## Children of Prosperity

Of those individuals growing up in the United States between 1946 and 1964, often referred to as children of post-war baby boom, the affluence of a profit-oriented system of free enterprise brought disenchantment and alienation to many. Although wealthy in terms of material items possessed, a significant number of individuals expressed their dissatisfaction and confusion by the social upheavals during the 60's and early 70's. Highly educated, yet critical of a system which bureaucracy exploited both its members inside and outside the system. Many individuals who grew up with the system's advantages found it lacking in providing the expected rewarding life.

Although rebellious in the area of individual morality, it remains a paradox that many were conscientious in the perspective of social morality as exemplified in recent social movements for ecology, peace, cooperative living.

Ever since the last industrial revolution, there has been a perpetual flow of Americans from the country to the city with the intent to upgrade and enrich their lifestyle. This mass movement of people to the urbanized areas has continued up until 1970 when suddenly it reversed. No longer satisfied with over crowded conditions, many Americans finally decided that a materialistic life was not for them. Pioneered by rural communes of the sixties, middle class Americans - in small numbers, began moving back to rural areas away from the fast paced urban life. Although most people today still live in cities or the immediate vicinity, polls have shown that 75% of these people would rather live in rural or small town communities. After years of urbanization, government over-regulation, and a disenchanted materialistic lifestyle, a growing minority of people have realized the necessity to get back to basics and have gained a renewed interest and desire in politics of decentralization with the emphasis on local popular control. Self-sufficiency has become the new mode for control over the immediate community environment. Problems can best be resolved and decisions made on the local level. "Small is beautiful" is probably the best caption able to illustrate this trend in living and thinking. "Good things come in small packages."

## The Hopi Way

Historically known as "Peaceful People," a name derived from their unique cultural orientation toward peace, the Hopi Indian tribe is an excellent model of an autonomous, self-sufficient community whose philosophical approach to life has enabled it to endure throughout centuries. Located approximately 70 miles north of Winslow, Arizona, in an area called Navajo Country, this unique southwestern Indian tribe has a stable agrarian-based economy supplemented by part-time craft work,

The World Book

**Oraibi,** a mutual enterprise community and built by the Hopi Indians during the 1100's, is probably the oldest continuously inhabited settlement in the United States.

pottery, basketry, weaving, and jewelry, one fifth which is kept, three fifths sold to tourists, and one fifth traded or sold through a complicated system of tribal exchange (Pueblo or Navajo). The Hopi Tribe, has maintained its heritage, ethics, social structure and technology untainted by foreign American influences even throughout the 20th century.

With a lifestyle orientation toward peace and happiness, the Hopi Way is founded on a philosophy that all things in life are intricately part of one single unit. Categories in our culture such as economic, social, and religious do not exist as separate entities in theirs. Instead, all facets of life, are interrelated under a simple set of rules and principles thus bringing the sacred and secular realm into one unit. Because the law of universal reciprocity reigns supreme under their philosophy, they believe all entities must cooperate together harmoniously for the welfare and survivability of the tribe.

*The real answers are not found in confrontation, or obstruction, or denying access, but rather in inclusion, cooperation, providing facts, and trying to build a common stake in the future.*

**~Author Unknown**

At the emotional and behavioral level, the Hopi Way is formulated into an integrated code of conduct regulating acting, feeling, and thinking. Because this code is collectively reinforced by public consensus, necessitated for group survival peculiar to their environmental conditions, one must constantly exercise self-control to insure that the Hopi Way is always exemplified.

### Socializing and Adjusting

The Hopis believe one must not experience such negative feelings as malice, fear, sadness or worry. One should endeavor to think good constructive thoughts followed by lawful and correct behavior. If one does not do so, ones personal endeavors will be unproductive and futile. To extend this concept even further, individual thoughts are believed to not only have a direct effect on physical objects but even on the general welfare of the entire community as well. Therefore, individual and tribal collective success and welfare are dependent on all members cultivating and practicing the Hopi Way at all times. One creates their own reality.

Despite the signs of a sick society, we need not give up hope and remain pessimistic thinking that doomsday will be reached before we were ever able to experience a UNISONIAN environment, an intermediate minimum entropy approach to building communities with the intent of non-entropic direction, a system for human and environmental excellence, A UNISONIAN MUTUAL ENTERPRISE SYSTEM.

I believe we can take solace if we come to the true understanding that wars, economic adversities and human misery occur simply because of wrong ways of thinking and living. In essence, we need a reconciliation between our means and our end.

### Reevaluation - A Plan for Reconstruction

If peace, happiness and plenty are the ideal unanimous characteristics of utopian state, an orderly progression from the first characteristic to the third cannot be reversed to reach the ultimate goal. As history so often demonstrates, peace and happiness cannot be found dependent on universal prosperity. In our centuries old battle to reverse this orderly process, the unequal accumulation and distribution of goods and intensified desire of wealth has not given us any greater inward harmony and satisfaction or real security. Rather, it has brought misery, desperation, and addiction, leaving people slaves to worldly rewards and their physical senses. What oriented toward the pursuit of goodness and virtue. A realization that spiritual health is necessary before one can truly experience the benefits of material desire to construct a system based on attention to the real needs of people, not to goods. An endeavor to create a new system of enterprise that considers the whole fullness of life. A decentralized system of control where local autonomy can best make their own decisions through the concept of what Loesch speaks of as UNISONIAN MUTUAL ENTERPRISE.

Until we determine with firm resolution to change direction from our present course, it is inevitable that we will continue to experience future sufferings and trials which serve to teach us the lessons of life. Events such as children killing other children for their brand name shoes or clothing, illustrates this point. It is my belief that only through understanding and application of true values, can we more quickly and successfully attain and experience a UNISONIAN state of affairs. Spirituality then, rather than economics, is the real key to prosperity as the following quotation best testifies, "People's characters are powerfully affected by the pattern of cultural characteristics of their society, and no element in the life of a society can do more to fix the pattern of its culture than its economic system--save only its religion (spirituality); which, in turn, if it is real, will involve an economic system compatible with it" (3:164) Within spirituality, therefore, must we find and structure an economic system based on the correct sequential steps of a UNISONIAN context, starting with peace, both inward and outward, before we can travel the true road to our universal dream of a utopian society.

# We Have Friends in High Places.

© 1992 FRANK OBERLE

*The Weak and the Strong*
*(Adaptation of Abraham Lincoln's Dissertation)*
*by Ivan L. Loesch*

*You can bring about prosperity ~*
*~ by encouraging thrift.*
*You can strengthen the weak ~*
*~ with the help of the strong.*
*You can help small men ~*
*~ with the help of big men*
*You can help the poor ~*
*~ with the help of the rich.*
*You can lift the wage earner ~*
*~ by working with the wage payer.*
*You can keep out of trouble ~*
*~ by not spending more than your income.*
*You can further brotherhood of man ~*
*~ by despising hatred.*
*You can establish sound security ~*
*~ with mutual investment.*
*You can build character and courage ~*
*~ by encouraging individual initiative.*
*You can really help people ~*
*~ by the Government helping them do*
*what they cannot do for themselves.*

# UNISONIA

## A BRIEF OVERVIEW OF THE BOOK

## UNISONIA
## THE UNISONIAN UNI-PARK/UNI-CITY PLAN
### IVAN L. LOESCH, DESIGNER-SPACE PLANNER

"If you want to change the world, there is no time like the present." That has been the activist's motto since time immemorial. This is the opening statement in the introduction of John Naisbitt and Patricia Aburdene's book REINVENTING THE CORPORATION. "But today. that advice is taking on new meaning. For several key reasons,

> *"Whatever you can do or dream you can, begin it. Boldness has genius, power and magic.*
> *~ Anonymous*

there really is no better time than now for reinventing our institutions----especially the corporations."

Many changes are being made in most of our social structures. This book is about taking action to make positive changes in the way we live our daily lives. I have outlined a new city prototype plan which reconciles freedom and order through an expanded Mutual Enterprise Economic System. New values and economic necessity will allow you to foster productive and fulfilling individual and family life in the new people-oriented environments.

Paul Tillich, points out very vividly what we are emphasizing in our work; "Humanity needs individuality and participation, dynamics and form, freedom and destiny." Alvin Pitcher in the Harvard Business Review, says "Humanity needs to participate meaningfully, find intentional, purposeful, disciplined direction around which his vitality can move; to find opportunity to deliberate and decide and be responsible for their own decisions and destiny."

A great percentage of the people of the world do not experience individuality and participation in the abundance of a purposeful and vital society.

*Destiny is not a matter of chance; it is a matter of choice.*
*~Anonymous*

For over thirty years I observed and studied living and housing methods of the past and the trends for the future. I have come to the conclusion that our present generations must take responsibility for reinventing the living patterns for the future. Innovative planners must take methods already invented and then apply them to create a systematic approach to solve people needs. I have thoroughly researched this subject and am supplying sources for all the progressive successful methods, activities and equipment I have incorporated in my plan, (spoken of here in general terms and more specifically in my thesis).

Environments form habits, therefore by designing appropriate people-oriented social and economic environments, positive, productive and socially beneficial habits will be formed, to a great degree for all the people experiencing that environment. Changing the environment also changes variables and the significance of them.

Cars, busses, planes, etc. are designed for a specific number of passengers. We don't allow 10 passengers to ride in a five passenger vehicle. We don't allow 300 passengers to ride in a 200 passenger plane. However, our cities don't fare so well; we allow more people to live in many areas than the areas can properly handle.

Many urban planners and sociologists say that communities of 8,000 to 10,000 population are an ideal size. My UNISONIAN plan is for 8,000 to 10,000 people like you to live in each Uni-City within a two mile square area. For more people within a larger area, clustering of Unit Cities can accomplish these unified plans.

My purpose is to develop this plan as a pattern for MUTUAL ENTERPRISE to bring many of the best people-oriented ideas together into a positive, realistic and workable socioeconomic plan for now and for the next century. A community where people work more closely together, as they do now in condominium, housing and park associations, group insurance and buying associations, corporate fleet, and quantity purchasing of equipment, vehicles and appliances. Unisonia is a corporation with real live shareholders, not a commune.

## "UNISONIA"

Samuel Butler's suggestion of a name for a nameless nation in his (Erewhon) was USONIA. Frank Lloyd Wright, the much heralded architect and planner, picked up on that name for his conceptual studies, writings and renderings about a more practical way of living. He proposed that each family in his community would live on a one acre lot, and that 14,000 families live on a 16 square mile tract. I believe Wright's plan spreads out the services and streets, to an impractical, financially unfeasible degree. This is why I have designed this community where every family has access to an eleven acre park on the other side of their patio gate - in the center of each twenty five acre Uni-Park. UNISONIA is the word I have chosen to represent the living plan described in the following information.

My emphasis is on the following:

Part I:    Creative Human Development

Part II:   Special concern is on the Environment and Land Use.

Part III:  Communication and Computerization

Part IV:   Administration which supports the Human and Environmental basis of our people-oriented community. In this day and time a large percentage of the people in the United States and the world are so occupied trying to make a living within a haphazard environment that they don't have the opportunity to really live.

**Part I. Creative Human Development** in the UNISONIAN UNI-CITI/ UNI-PARK system offers a wholesome, quality environment, community participation, equity stock ownership and the opportunity for individual growth, development and self esteem to take place within a creative, warm, positive and exciting atmosphere.

Good health is assured through proper nutrition education, balanced recreation and elimination of chemical pollutants.

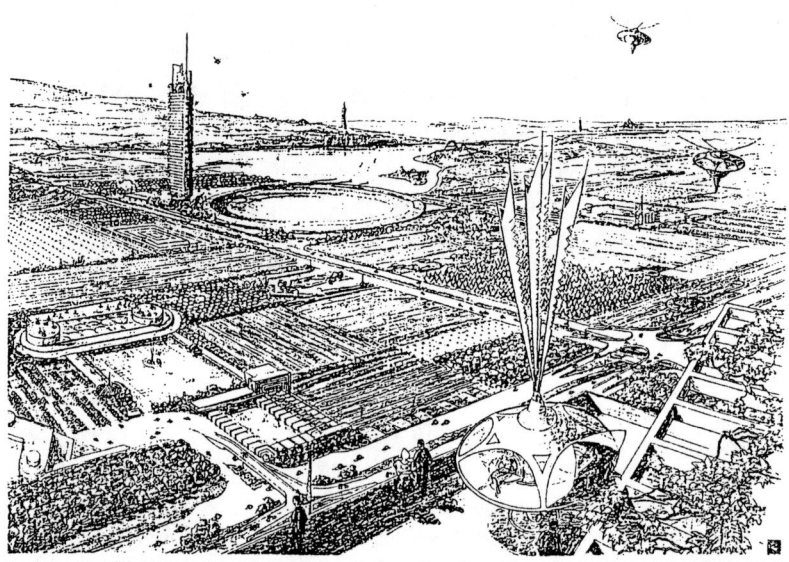

The city-as-machine: This philosophy of urban planning can be traced back to Broadacres, Frank Lloyd Wright's suburban interpretation of the American Dream that emphasized individualism over community. "Because we have the automobile," wrote Wright, "we can go far and fast. ...houses [can now] be a quarter of a mile apart [instead of] ten to a block ...I have always referred to this as the architecture of democracy: the freedom of the individual becomes the motive." Presumably, Wright's vision did *not* include strip malls, ozone holes, or rush hour gridlock.

The city as machine: This philosophy of urban planning can be traced back to Broadacres, Frank Lloyd Wright's suburban interpretation of the American Dream that emphasized individualism over community. "Because we have the automobile," wrote Wright, "we can go far and fast...houses (can now be a quarter of a mile apart (instead of) ten to a block....I have always referred to this as the architecture of democracy; the freedom of the individual becomes the motive." Presumably, Wright's vision did *not* include strip malls, ozone holes, or rush hour gridlock.

The mental well being of the uni-citizen is accomplished by providing wholesome growth and eliminating hassles in a restful, peaceful, but fertile, environment. Other services are offered such as administrative assistance, seminars and other services to further human growth potential.

Each UNI-PARK has trails and numerous other physical recreational use spaces. The growth centers in each UNI-PARK also provide many health building offerings. Visualize the fun and exciting activities of the many children playing games, adults and children jogging, riding trikes and bikes on the paved trail. Its great to see all the picnickers enjoying all the things to do in the parks.

A view inside the UNI-PARK

The UNI-CITI is formed around a unique caring attitude with safety built in. The twenty eight neighborhoods provide parks to all 10,000 citizens of the community without crossing a street. Each home uses fire proof and fire resistant materials and other state of-the-art smart house equipment as much as possible. All security needs are administered and assisted through the central administrative and design offices to make the community as safe as possible.

The cultural development of the community will grow because of the many nationalities active within the community. Musical and artistic activities make fulfilled, peaceful and exuberant, positive emotions real to everyone.

## JUSTICE = PEACE

UNISONIANS ENCOURAGE
A SUSTAINABLE ENVIRONMENT
WHICH WILL FOSTER PEACE through the
WORLDWIDE "Transition to Peace" Movement.

GET INVOLVED -
SPEAK UP for JUSTICE,
LIVE for PEACE

The "Transition to Peace" is sponsored by
The World Economic Forum
Klaus Schwab Founder and President
Phone: 202-456-2326

(Picture D)

Unisonia High School Upper Level Citi-Centre Dimension-Summer 1988

The UNI-CITI plan encourages individual and collective spiritual growth within the community. Churches are encouraged to lease and share facilities such as space and parking lots from the UNI-CITI Corporation as well as make use of the closed circuit cable system and other media.

*Education makes a people easy to lead, but difficult to drive; easy to govern, but impossible to enslave.*

~ **Lord Brougham**

Because "we are what we know," UNISONIA is the ultimate educational opportunity to develop the minds of all uni-citizens. Life for everyone is constantly an education toward greater fulfillment mentally as well as remunerative monetarily. The preschool and elementary kids will go to the UNI-PARK Association Growth Centers and also use the home computer center in all the homes within the UNI-CITI. Secondary grades are housed in the UNI-CITI CENTRE where the students become directly involved in business experience as well as other varied services within the center. Everyone tries to make all experiences during work or leisure times, creative, enjoyable, fulfilling and beneficial to the adult individuals growth in UNISONIA as well.

**Part II. Sensible Environmental Land Use** is directly associated with successful human activity. The attitude of UNISONIA is one of conservation and experimentation of practices which benefit both uni-citizens and the environment. Just think of the happiness you can experience within such an environment.

Resources creatively managed can provide a multitude of benefits monetarily, recreationally, agriculturally and for beautification.

Water, both domestic potable and environmental is taken very seriously, with special care in properly using this valuable resource to eliminate unnecessary processing, contamination and handling, making more and better use of less water through control flow shower heads, automatic shutoffs, and community education.

Environmentally, drip irrigation and hydroponics will be used primarily watering only areas intended to be watered. Lakes and streams may be lined to keep from losing water to seepage.

Picture this, the lakes and streams are stocked with fish, making the lakes and streams more enjoyable. Swans, geese and ducks make the lakes their home. Aesthetic landscaping enhances surrounding areas.

What in most instances is considered waste and of no value can be profitably processed and provide not only financial value from sale of materials but also employment value.

Water entering the household is potable drinking water for use in many ways; however, clothes washing and bathing water is filtered and recycled for use in flushing effluent from a two quart flush toilet, saving about fifty to sixty gallons of water per family unit each day multiplying to 45.6 millions of gallons per year not needing expensive processing. In this community of 10,000 the completely filtered water draining from the effluent processing systems are used for underground drip watering of private or public vegetation.

Effluent is recycled for useable compost and methane. Other waste materials such as metal, glass, plastic and paper are separated by each household and placed in separate containers within two hundred feet of each home unit. Effluent, which is a big concern in any community, can through proper recycling become a profitable, positive value-producing substance.

Uni-Sonians make use of known agricultural methods in areas provided within and/or adjacent to the UNI-CITI similar to the rental gardens in Europe. The year around practice of hi density planting of vegetables and irrigating with nutrient supplement for fast healthy plant growth is encouraged.

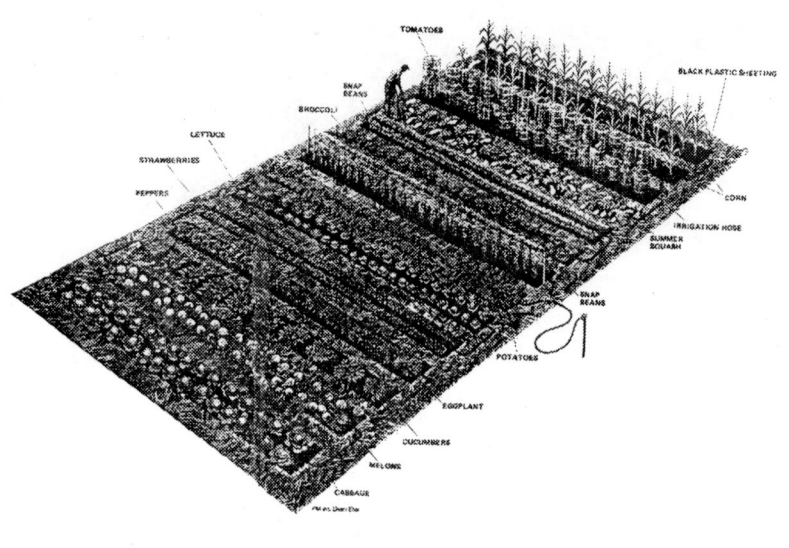

Several methods of home and commercial production providing fresh nutritional foods in the UNI-SONIAN Citi make use of agricultural production and processing methods to provide nutritional foods at economical costs while at the same time providing job opportunities for uni-citizen shareholders through hydroponics, greenhouses, trees, shrubs and multi-use crops. Selected fruit trees and berry plants provide a lot of pleasure, beauty and dessert.

The constancy of solar energy availability makes it imperative that this natural resource be used in whatever ways possible. Research and experimentation is recommended and encouraged. Park, yard and street lighting are only three practical uses for solar voltaics. All house and public roofs provide space for electric generation panels. UNISONIA is a proto-type community for any solar voltaic experiments that hold potential such as passive and active heat generation for both public and private spaces, preheating water for domestic use, auto washing and swimming pools as well as other uses like ag and waste processing.

Transportation, the orderly movement of people, vehicles and materials are important for safety, sound control, general tranquility and well being. All bridges, streets and motorways are designed for maximum efficiency, aesthetics and safety, We are using places like San Antonio, Texas' River Walk as an example.

The landscape beauty of UNISONIA is fantastic, with total community landscape design. Uni-citizens are provided landscape design assistance as well as provisions for economical plantings provided by the commercial ag production service within the UNI-CITI.

Landscaping around lakes, streams, waterfalls, motorways, parking areas and buffer areas are aesthetically pleasing and help create a pleasant community atmosphere. A small lake and a waterfall are also located in each UNI-PARK. The UNI-PARK people-land ratio is three and one half homesites per acre which is not a heavy ratio.

Each UNI-PARK association administers all aspects of their respective UNI-PARK. Each unit owner has one vote in the affairs of their own UNI-PARK and the UNI-CITI; therefore, everyone has equal input opportunity.

Author Loesch enjoying a walking tour of The River Walk, San Antonio, Texas

Uni-Citizens are provided landscape design assistance

**Part III. Communications and Computerization** in part three tie everything together and includes entertainment, security and public information. One of the most important considerations in any concept, organization or group is open communication. The UNISONIAN Master Plan is designed to make maximum use of the numerous media available in order to offer fulfilling growth opportunities whenever possible through educational TV, computerization, video library, the printed media and radio. New communication equipment is constantly being developed to provide updated capability, thereby providing expanded services. Administrative planning services are practicably networked into the citi wide communication system.

**Part IV.    Administrative Services.** Every successful enterprise must possess capable and conscientious management personnel. UNISONIA draws farsighted, creative, positive minded, people-oriented management because of the terrific, exciting creative challenges it projects.

The basic administration of the UNISONIAN UNI-CITI is a mutual cooperative, nonprofit, shareholder corporation which owns the public aspects of the community but all home lots are privately owned. Each lot owner holds one share of stock in the UNI-CITI corporation. A Board of Directors, elected one from each UNI-Quad and one from the commercial and service zones administers the city through a trained city manager. Personnel come from the shareholder population as much as possible.

A representative from each of the seven UNI-PARKS within each UNI-QUAD coordinates activities within the UNI-QUAD and also serves on the UNI-CITI Advisory Board.

Financially, UNISONIA may join with a large investment banking establishment, large insurance company and/or other financial entity in order to purchase land, to lay out streets, water, electric, cable, telephone lines, etc. through a developer. The developer constructs the streams and lakes and establishes the nucleus businesses and production facilities in the UNI-CITI CENTRE.

Structures and facilities are designed through the Administrative Office of Planning with the assistance of computer-aided design systems, the purpose of which is to provide maximum useability, economy and practical space use while having pleasing aesthetic input by staff designers and Uni-Citizens.

Approximately one third of the price of the lot is a shareholders equity purchase for corporate stock in the business facilities of UNISONIA. This investment establishes leveraging funds for immediate business building, including economical small shops and service spaces.

Since the purchasing department can obtain building materials and appliances in larger quantities, the savings are passed on to the corporate shareholder/Uni-citizens through lease of Fleet purchased vehicles as well as other large purchases.

UNISONIA marketing of its products attracts the interest of people world wide because of the way it addresses the needs

Unisonia maintains productive and creative manufacturing associates

of individuals and families now. The concept is promoted and offered to anyone who wants to be a productive part in an affordable contemporary pacesetting community.

Economic development is accomplished through manufacturing the many products needed in building the many houses plus the kitchen and bathroom cabinets, concrete and wood fence, patio deck blocks, stair units and all the other items needed to be manufactured will keep many people employed. Other people-friendly and environment-friendly industries are welcomed.

The UNI-CENTRE is started in the early stages of UNISONIA. This creates employment for the shareholders.

The Realty Service Division of the corporation coordinates the sale of lots and works in close proximity with administration.

Invention, innovation research, development and industrial productivity are considered very important to create continued growth in employment as well as economic growth. The world view demands that care be taken in every aspect of life to protect the most fragile micro-organisms to the largest creatures and plants still growing on this planet and within the universe. People can no longer continue to pillage and rape the earth without significant damage to the universal system thereby multiplying its negative effects. The time has come for all people of the earth to unite in allowing the innate care humanity has within its self for nature, freeing the abundant life and allowing it to flow through all people

*"When society (nature) prospers, the individual will prosper."*

~ *Anonymous*

of the earth. We are at a time when we must achieve more with less, a philosophy espoused by futurist Buckminister Fuller.

Significant power is present within the universe to orchestrate many a symphony made up of very diverse attitudes into the sounds and vibrations that become a positive song of all people. This music encourages, motivates and excites humanity to free the positive, magnificent energy bound up in people around the world to sing, walk, work, and play in harmony so that the music which can be created by all may be enjoyed by all. Care is a key word. A commitment to open empathetic caring is the life blood of Unisonia, an attitude of self determination, confidence and sharing the wealth of the universe.

I challenge you to become a player in UNISONIA.

You may keep tuned into UNISONIA and receive a complete copy of UNISONIA including sources by sending $24.95 by credit card or money order to:

Ivan Loesch/Unisonia Institute
Box 1374
Huron, South Dakota 57350-1374.

Refer to pages 217-219 for complete ordering details.

**UNISONIA**
**Index Preamble**

## UNI-CITI COMMUNITY SUCCESS FACTORS

Human Factors:
  Providing Health Care;
  Strong Multi-Generational Family Orientation
  Deliberate Integration Of Power Between Generations
  Of Leaders
  Acceptance Of Women In Leadership Roles
  Strong Belief In And Support For Education

Environmental And Land Use:
  Evidence Of Community Pride
  Emphasis On Quality In Business And Community Life
  Sound And Well-Maintained Infrastructure

Communications And Computerization:
  Sophisticated Use Of Information Resources.
  Strong Presence Of Traditional Institutions That Are
  Integral To Community Life
  Participatory Approach To Community Decision Making
  Cooperative Community Spirit

Administrative Services:
  Conviction That In The Long Run, You Have To Do It
  Yourself
  Willingness To Seek Help From Outside
  Active Economic Development Program.

Careful Use Of Fiscal Resources
Willingness To Invest In The Future
Realistic Appraisal Of Future Opportunities
Awareness Of Community Positioning
Knowledge Of The Physical Environment

Value Statements:
Everyone Has Something To Contribute
Everyone Needs Meaningful Relationships
People Deserve The Dignity Of Making Choices
Life Is Meant To Be Enjoyed by All

# BUY RECYCLED.

# AND SAVE.™

Thanks to you, all sorts of everyday products are being made from recycled materials. But to keep recycling working, you need to buy those products. For a free brochure, call 1-800-CALL-EDF.

 A Public Service of This Publication

©1994 EDF

# THE UNISONIAN UNI-PARK/UNI-CITI PLAN
Ivan L. Loesch, Inventor, Designer-Space Planner

# PART I
## HUMAN POTENTIAL

### A. CREATIVE HUMAN DEVELOPMENT

In this day and time, a large percentage of the people in the United States and the world are so occupied at making a living that they don't have the opportunity to really live.

A method must be initiated to allow people the option to pattern their lives in such a way that the basic hopes and dreams of all may be pursued with hope of achievement.

Everyone needs opportunities to create. Unisonian life is designed to encourage, nurture and launch the creative process for all Uni-Citians, in a positive environment.

The community will encourage the attitude of fulfilled living without the extreme pressures of success based on material excess but rather on caring service to others, the challenge of excellence, of attitude, personality and style.

# UNI-CITI COMMUNITY SUCCESS FACTORS
Patterned after The Heartland Center for Leadership Development in Lincoln, Nebraska. (by Val Farmer, Ph.D.)

## HUMAN FACTORS:

### Providing Health Care.
Local health care is a common concern. The focus may be in emergency medical services or investing heavily in comprehensive hospital based services.

### Strong Multi-Generational Family Orientation.
These are family-oriented communities, with activities often built around family needs and ties, where true familial love and agape love (brotherly love) between people, and a place where romance continues after marriage.

### Deliberate Integration of Power Between Generations of Leaders.
Integrated leadership is the rule more than the exception in thriving communities. People of all ages hold key positions in civic and business affairs.

### Acceptance of Women in Leadership Roles.
Women are often found in key leadership and managerial positions such as mayor/citi manager, Uni-park directors, department managers, executive officers of health care facilities, developers of entrepreneurial ventures, or as presidents of community enterprises and service organizations.

**Strong Belief in and Support for Education.**

Good schools are a point of pride as well as a stable employment force. Residents want their children to get the best education they can afford. Beyond that, the school is often a center of social activity. Sporting, cultural and other school events are well attended.

**PART II**
**ENVIRONMENTAL AND LAND USE:**

**Evidence of Community Pride.**

UNI-CITI communities are places of community attention with cared-for yards, public vegetable and flower gardens, and well-kept parks. But pride also shows up in other ways, especially in community festivals and events in which the community celebrates its history and heritage.

**Emphasis on Quality in Business and Community Life.**

People in UNI-CITI communities believe that something worth doing is worth doing right. Facilities and homes are built to last, as long and longer than the 50 years as outlined in presently accepted codes. The community always makes use of recently developed energy-conserving and structural materials in combination with other aesthetically desirable materials such as stone, wood, thatch and earth.

**Sound and Well-Maintained Infrastructure.**

UNI-CITI communities place importance on maintaining and improving their streets, sidewalks, water system, and sewage treatment facilities.

## PART III
## COMMUNICATIONS AND COMPUTERIZATION:

### Sophisticated use of Information Resources.

UNI-CITI community leaders learn about trends and changes that affect their community by using data generated outside their community (retail sales histories, census data, application of computer technology, etc.)

### Strong Presence of Traditional Institutions that are Integral to Community Life.

Churches and schools could help provide a focus for community activities. Active service clubs are a strong positive communicative influence in the community.

### Participatory Approach to Community Decision Making.

Power is deliberately shared in these communities. Even the most powerful opinion leaders seem to work through the systems--formal as well as informal--to build understanding and appreciation for what they want to do.

### Cooperative Community Spirit.

More attention is devoted to cooperative activities rather than concern about what should be done and by whom. The stress is on working together toward a common goal, and the focus is on positive results through active communication.

## PART IV
## ADMINISTRATIVE SERVICES:

### Conviction that, in the long run, "Communities have to Do It Themselves."

UNI-CITI communities believe their destiny is in their own hands. They are not waiting for someone else to save them, nor do they believe that "things will turn out" if they sit back and wait. They are pro-active in making their communities a good place to live.

### Willingness to Seek Help from the Outside.

UNI-CITI communities demonstrate their success by competing for government and private grants and contracts that will develop their local resources.

### Active Economic Development Program.

An organized and active approach to economic development is common in successful communities. Public and private groups coordinate their interests. Private economic development firms are common.

### Careful Use of Fiscal Resources.

Conservation is a way of life and expenditures are made carefully. However, people will spend money, and when they do, the things they buy are built to last. Improvements are seen as investments in the future of the community. Care has been taken to solve needs creatively by use of modern materials when practical.

### Willingness to Invest in the Future.

Residents invest time and energy in community betterment. They concern themselves with the impact -- how and what they are doing today will influence both their lives and those of their children and grandchildren in the future.

**Realistic Appraisal of Future Opportunities.**

These communities build on strengths and minimize weaknesses. The emphasis is on building the community from within by home-grown business expansion and retention by mutual venture investment by all property owner/shareholders.

**Awareness of Community Positioning.**

Thriving communities know how to compete, and so do the businesses in the communities, Everyone tries to emphasize local loyalty as a way to assist local businesses. They are concerned about what they don't have locally. They want hometown folks to have every opportunity to shop locally.

**Knowledge of the Physical Environment.**

Importance of location is underscored continually in local decision-making. Community leaders are aware of the natural and human resources available locally.

**VALUE STATEMENTS:**
**Everyone has Something to Contribute.**

Each person, regardless of physical or intellectual ability has something he or she can teach or give to others. For this reason, each person is unique and deserves to be valued and respected. This basic value and respect does not depend on one's economic status, intellect, potential for productivity, or other traits or attributes but is inherent.

Seeking to uncover and encourage each other's special gifts is everyone's job. Holding the perspective that all human beings are unique and valuable frees us to focus on the positive and will not only encourage growth in others, but will simultaneously enrich and expand ourselves. This is something that must be taught by example and learned from childhood, (just like prejudices are).

### Everyone Needs Meaningful Relationships.

Of the most elemental needs we all have is to love and be loved and to form meaningful relationships. We are most healthy and happy when we are interdependent. Building relationships takes attention, effort, and commitment. Our relationship need not always be built on affection, but can and should be built on respect.

Positive, caring relationships cannot be forced but can and should be encouraged. By helping each other develop the skills and attitudes which enhance our ability to form such relationships, we enable others to become more whole and fulfilled. We must keep a respectful awareness of the role relationship plays in giving our lives meaning.

### People Deserve the Dignity of Making Choices.

It is by experiencing the consequences of our choices that we achieve our greatest growth. Each person deserves the opportunity to take risks and make choices to succeed and to fail. It is often through a perceived failure that we learn life's most important messages.

We need to encourage each other to take responsible risks, to appreciate and expand our capacity to make choices and to accept and learn from the consequences of our actions. Enhancing other's abilities and opportunities to choose for themselves is one of the most respectful gifts we can give.

# LOESCH

**Life is Meant to be Enjoyed.**

There is humor in almost everything if we care to seek it. Humor alone cannot diminish life's difficulties, but it can do much to help us get through them. By sharing our joys, as well as our sorrows, we create a positive, happy atmosphere which will, in turn, nourish and energize those with whom we come in contact.

We must provide each other opportunities to laugh and have fun, both in planned activities, and as we go about our daily lives. Life is too short and too precious not to fully enjoy it.

**Creative Human Development**

The UNISONIAN UNI-CITI/UNI-PARK system offers a wholesome environment, community participation, ownership and the opportunity for individual growth and development to take place within a creative, positive atmosphere. People will be encouraged with numerous opportunities to participate and grow as they develop personal as well as Unisonian concepts, ideas and innovations for the exuberant feeling of personal satisfaction and also the potential of personal financial gain. As an example, all UNISONIANS are challenged to creatively initiate economic development concepts, products and marketing of production of the UNISONIAN community.

**1. Health**

The basics of good health will be fostered through proper nutrition education for all ages. Balanced recreation and elimination of chemical pollutants within the community will allow for better health for all people realizing that much of the pollutants people endure are from outside the UNI-CITI.

8

UNISONIANS will actively work politically toward elimination of such polluting sources.

Uni-Citizens will be surrounded by good mental and physical health reinforcers so individuals and families will find it more enjoyable to eliminate unnecessary unhealthy actions.

Everyone will receive training and encouragement to eat nourishing foods, have organic growth of vegetables in the community and establish positive emotional support systems.

Clinical care facilities will be located within the Uni-Citi in the service park area. The newest methods making use of such technology as computer tie in to each house for health and nutrition will be implemented. A hospital will be placed in the Uni-Citi when feasible. Until that time, hospital services will be provided within the metro. Emergency and regular clinical care will be provided within the community as well as emergency ambulatory transportation to acute care facilities outside the Uni-Citi.

There is an emerging health paradigm that focuses on the individual versus institutional responsibility for health. Uni-Citi health professionals will help seniors develop beliefs, skills and resources necessary to promote this change, and demonstrate how the empowerment process is used to help senior gain control over their own health care.

•"Health Promotion: Impact of Empowering the Aging American" # 1

UNISONIA will provide a challenging opportunity to explore a linking approach to a community oriented respite care program. Professionals working with the elderly, specifically the Alzheimer person and caregiver, are exposed to an innovative program, utilizing healthy senior citizens in a neighbor -helping-neighbor approach to providing direct in-home respite care services. The community will provide enhanced service to residents by connecting with the special needs youth population in the community, illustrating how physically/emotionally disabled youth and youthful offenders can foster mutual growth and healing through ongoing service and sharing with residents.

•Intergenerational Services # 2

Health professionals will help seniors gain knowledge and skills to enhance care for older persons with developmental disabilities. These include knowledge about emotional and social needs, friendship patterns, training in legal issues, including potential liability and regulatory trend, and behavioral guidelines on managing behavior.

•"Enhancing Services for Developmentally Disabled residents in Nursing Homes" # 3

## a. Mental Well-Being

The mental well being of the Uni-Citizen is a primary consideration in the development of the UNI-CITI plan, providing wholesome growth and eliminating hassles as much as possible in all aspects of the master plan. Each Uni-Citizen has easy access to over two hundred acres of parks or wilderness area.

•Meditation Gardens # 4
•Waterfalls provide restful enjoyment. # 5

Welcome to "The Medicine of the Future!" scientific accounts tell us most people use only about 10% of their brain. Geniuses like Albert Einstein only utilized about five percent more. We can only wonder about what potential lies in the untapped 90 percent.

Scientists and brain researchers are now saying that it is possible to tap more of the unused portion of our brain and use it to heal faster...learn more easily...achieve more...stay healthier...live longer...even look younger!

The best health advice one can give or receive is: *watch out for stress*! Scientists are finding that unchecked stress is a major factor in triggering or causing many of today's serious diseases, including cancer, heart trouble, high blood pressure, stroke, even herpes.

It's time to take stress seriously, to learn how to avoid it, defuse it, and protect yourself from its effects. Because this world of ours is becoming increasingly stressful. *The ability to effectively relieve stress is going to be an essential survival skill* for you and me, our children and our friends.

•A guidebook/complimentary cassette is available. **# 6**

A Medical Revolution -- You and I and the medical community are poised on the threshold of a medical revolution that promises to radically change our understanding of disease, health, and the healing process forever. And if you feel yourself getting excited about the new possibilities these discoveries hold for your personal health and the health of those you love, you are not alone!

As one enthusiastic researcher said: "The field of psychoneuroimmunology (literally: using the mind to heal the body) holds the most promise for our medical future."

A physician who has explored this amazing power says, "the true medical frontier lies within the individual."

You are invited to take a practical look at what this excitement is about -- to see how to tap the sleeping powers of your brain to get more of what you want from life.

The Complete Guide To Your Emotions and Your Health -- a book filled with new scientific, medical and psychiatric findings that radically change our ideas of illness and health forever is available from Radial books and is on our star reading list.

*"Good instincts usually tell you what to do long before your head has figured it out."*

**~ Michael Burke**

We will be hearing and learning more about homeopathy -- the method of treating diseases by very small doses of drugs, which in large doses would produce in a healthy person symptoms similar to those of the disease.

Naturopathic Technologies work with natural remedies such as manipulation, homeopathy and physical therapy.

Use of homeopathic remedies may be new to you although its use dates back centuries, even thousands of years.

Homeopathic therapy consists of giving the patient an infinitesimal dose of a natural substance from either the PLANT kingdom (ex. an herb), or the MINERAL kingdom (ex. a natural salt), or from the ANIMAL kingdom (ex. a hormone).

This will have an effect on the patient according to the Law of Similars which is to cure a patient of a (similar) (HOMEO) (suffering) (PATHOS). Homeopathic remedies have no toxicity, no side effects, and are non-addictive. They cause the body to "react and cure itself" of the problem it needs trying to overcome.

Homeopathic remedies are not medicines. Their role is that of a catalyst: to initiate a process without becoming a part of it.

Homeopathies is commonly used all over the world. In England, the Royal Family regularly uses homeopathy. In France, nearly every pharmacy carries homeopathic remedies. India has a particular affinity for homeopathy's approach to disease and the patient. Mahamda Gandhi declared, "Homeopathy cures a larger percentage of cases than any other method of treatment and is beyond all doubt safer, more economical and the most complete medical science."

The program offers the latest in alternative health care and should be used to complement existing, proven medical techniques. It consists of the examination through some very special diagnostic equipment. First of all, a comprehensive case history and symptom survey form are completed. Then with a research grade darkfield microscope, blood is analyzed for the following.

1. Detailed and individualized programming for diet, exercise and appropriate vitamin and mineral supplementation.
2. Assessment of the impact of environmental pollution on the blood and immune system.
3. Allergenic responses.
4. Identification of iron deficiency and tendencies toward anemia.
5. Identification of the effect of stress on the immune and circulatory systems.

Besides standard blood and urine analysis, the most exciting part of the testing is done with a revolutionary new machine called the VEGATEST. It uses methods called the Bio-Electric regulatory technique which was developed by scientists in Germany who used ELECTRO-Acupuncture for diagnosis. The VEGATEST evaluates the following:

1. Energetical Weaknesses (ex. Pituitary, Adrenal, Thyroid.)
2. Physiological Weaknesses (ex. Heart, Lungs, Kidney, Liver.)
3. Chemical Toxicities (ex. Insecticides, Herbicides, Paint and Cleaning Solvents, Food Additives.)
4. Viral and Bacterial Contaminations (ex. Staph, Strep, Candida.)
5. Food and Heavy Metal Poisoning (ex. Lead, Mercury, Arsenic.)
6. Latent/Toxic Effects of Drugs, Antibiotics, and Immunizations.
7. Inflammatory Conditions (ex. Gout, Arthritis, Rheumatoid Arthritis, Kidney, Bladder,)

The purpose is to:

1. Give understanding to the cause of disease and the way back to health.
2. Detoxify specific toxins and eliminate their negative effect on the body.
3. Rebuild the body using homeopathic remedies, herbs, nutrients and exercise.
4. Give specific diet and fluid intake recommendations.
5. Involve, and stress the need for, certain other programs such as chiropractic and acupuncture.
6. Give other recommendations too numerous to mention.

•Homeopathy - the Complete Guide To Your Emotions And Your Health. # 7

## b. Physical Activity, Recreation and Leisure

It was Thoreau who said, "Now and then be idle, sit and think." A good trend of thought at such a time is, "What is my status? Am I a good friend of mankind so I have more friends? Have I more friends than I had a year ago? A month ago? Any fewer enemies? Am I doing better work on my job? Am I meeting my greater responsibilities to myself and those who believe in me?" Now and then be idle--and just sit and think!

> *"Everywhere is walking distance if you have the time."*
> ~*Steven Wright*

Each UNI-PARK has a 1.25 mile, 6 foot wide trail for walking, biking and other use as well as providing ball fields and numerous other physical recreational use spaces such as swimming pools, shuffle board courts, and horseshoe courts. Biking and jogging trails are also available beside the canal for canoeing and paddle boating within seven blocks of everyone. The growth centers in each UNI-PARK also provide many offerings.

ILLUSTRATIONS BY HUNT ASSOCIATES/STEVE SCHLENKER

Many other avenues of relaxation are available to everyone in these communities, most would fit into the ten following categories.

The ten areas of community recreation providing a total relaxing, invigorating, "ahhh" experience are:

1. Sports and games
2. Art
3. Drama
4. Special events
5. Aquatics
6. Dance and aerobics
7. Music

8.     Outdoor activities
9.     Literature
10.    Crafts

ILLUSTRATIONS BY HUNT ASSOCIATES/STEVE SCHLENKER

A balance of active/passive, indoor/outdoor, competitive/ noncompetitive, classes/day workshops, leagues/team play (team - learning how to socialize, individual - self discipline), open gym/special events, cost/free, short term programs/on going ones will be emphasized.

•Outdoor Learning Centers # 8

Psycho-social rehabilitation with the older population is based on the premise that success in work, self-care, and leisure is critical to mental well-being. It is important to explore and develop new skills and maintain current skills that are required for adaptation to the physical and emotional process of aging and to the requirements of a changing lifestyle.

•The goal of program planning is to evaluate functioning and facilitate optimal performance in areas of recognition, social /interpersonal skills, self-care, and leisure activities. #9

## 2. Safety - Security

The 28 UNI- PARKS which provide parks to all 10,000 citizens of the community without crossing a street, provides added safety. Non-property owners may enter a UNI-PARK commons as a guest. The UNI-CITI is formed around a unique caring attitude with built in safety.

## a. Fire Protection

Each home will have automatic interior fire extinguishing and alarm systems and also water at the back of the lot. Fire proof and fire resistant materials and methods will be used as much as possible in all buildings.

A state of the art emergency alert system is distributed to seniors and the disabled.

•The program is sponsored nationally by the International Association of firefighters and Muscular Dystrophy Association. #10

## b. General Security and Peace Keeping

All security needs will be administered through the central

administrative office making use of the closed circuit TV scanning of all UNI-PARKS. Security persons under each UNI-PARK Association, the UNI-CENTRE and Service Zone will complement the over all peace-keeping activity.

The community must determine the use of guns within the UNI-CITI. Police can be a weapon, just like guns. The community must diligently strive to ensure that security does not become oppressive, a benevolent slavery.

The community will recognize the potential for mind control and therefore will work hard to keep new ideas from being destroyed.

Informative video and other methods of positive attitude reinforcers will be used. For example, A Youth Safety Watch Action Team (SWAT) encourages and assists young people to understand and become adept at recognizing potential hazards and also potential beneficial actions for Uni-Citians.

### 3. Cultural Enhancement

The cultural development of the community will grow in all areas of the arts. Many opportunities for cultural development and growth will take place through the many nationalities represented within the community.

International and ethnic celebrations will highlight the rich interrelationships fostered within the community. Historical, Humanities, and other societies are a vital part of these communities.

I propose the identification of all possible Project Grant Proposals, Fellowships, etc., for organizations, rural and small communities. Other programs of interest which can possibly be incorporated into prototype Unisonian communities such as those sponsored through the auspices of the National Endowment for the Arts, National Science Foundation, National Science Center - Fort Gordon, Georgia, and other educational foundations should be plugged into The National Educational Association who encourages Visual Arts, Museums, Media Arts (film/radio/television,) Arts in Education, Expansion Arts, Inter-Arts, Local Programs, and N.E.A. administration fellows, Challenge Grants, Advancement Programs, Office for Special Constituencies (Activities to Older Adults,) International Activities should also be researched.

Likewise, there are many other programs through state and federal government auspices, foundations and other organizations which are potentially applicable for use in a prototype Unisonian community.

## a. Artistic

Why Public Art? Not since the 1930's with the WPA (Works Progress Administration) programs has there been such interest and concern in providing art for the public in public places.

Public art will give the Uni-Citi a sense of its culture which contributes to community pride and prestige and defines identity for both citizens and visitors, preserving through art, its past and present. No group benefits more than the children.

Picture-perfect Montmartre

Artists and artwork will be selected by the Arts Council based on recommendations from a panel specifically chosen for each project.

Our artists and the artworks they create reflect our culture, our history and our future. Their works are the Lasting Legacy we leave our children. Though governments, economies and people change, the vision of the artist survives to be handed down from generation to generation. The creative foundation of the community

21

provides much encouragement and opportunity for all uni-citizens to experience the creative process through numerous means as close as each UNI-CITI Growth Centre, UNI-PARK and the UNI-CITI CENTRE.

Opportunity for learning many forms of artistic expression such as painting, sculpturing, photography, video, creative writing and many more arts and crafts will be available.

Cameos of older adults advocating for intergenerational arts and structured continuing education that motivates and stimulates intergenerationally will be encouraged.
•Intergenerational Encounters with the Arts **# 11**

## b. Music

Much opportunity for musical expression will take place fostering peace, exuberance and the many other positive emotions.

Acting Up! is a nationally acclaimed performing troupe of older adults, who, using their own original material, sing, dance and humor their way through the myths, stereotypes of aging. The group taped a video before a live studio audience. Their Artistic Director Joyce Stern Greenberg encourages drama activities and ideas for use with groups of varying levels of ability as a means of motivating and inspiring creativity with older adults.
•The 60- minute Acting Up video **# 12**

## 4. Individual and Family Life

People need to feel in control of their lives. They need love, commitment, communications, and open-hearted, humorous good friends. UNISONIA will make every effort to make these and other human attributes as easy as possible to achieve.

In the Uni Citi plan, human values are the bottom line. The threads of human values are woven throughout the system. People will strive to live within a system which allows for great creativity, variety and individuality. The system is intended to eliminate as much as possible the numerous present pitfalls, difficulties, traps, and wastes which misdirect and mislead so many because of lack of creative structure and creative discipline.

Oregon State Senior Services Division, Sponsor:

Description: Results of a year-long demonstration project indicate that quality of life can be maintained and enhanced through proper assessment of personalized goal development. Personalizing quality of life issues may be the key to optimizing the institutionalized aging client's functioning and ADLS (Activities of Daily Living) psychosocial well-being, and health promotion. **# 13**

Presbyterian Homes of New Jersey/Project LINC. Sponsor.

Description: Long term care systems bridge the gap from independence to interdependence. Community service partnerships, alternative and adaptive living environments, and adult day care are some of the choices that will help prepare for the future. **#14**

State Farm Insurance

## a. Personal Management and Career Development

Highly appropriate for each individual, adult and youth alike, is to aspire to a well-directed life. Principles of good personal

24

management can be learned at an early age and will be offered to all UNI-Citizens through educational video, library and other presentations.

### b. Financial Planning

Money Management -- With knowledgeable guidance, anyone can develop good money management skills. All that is required is a few hours initially and periodic review and adjustment. It is simple but is not easy because it requires self discipline. The benefits can be enormous: freedom from financial worries...a better lifestyle...and life long financial security. The Financial Planning Centers provide a free Seminar series on all aspects of money management. They have the latest in financial planning technology through the Financial Planning Software System and Computer Centers. Trained Account Executives will be happy to work with individuals in analyzing one's current financial condition and develop an implementation plan to assist in obtaining all that you wish to achieve financially.

The Financial Planning Centers are dedicated to serving the needs and desires of the community through professional financial planning. They will review your situation on a personal basis and design a program that meets your needs and desires and those of your family.

•Financial Planning Centers # **15**


## B. SPIRITUAL ENHANCEMENT

The UNI-CITI plan encourages individual and collective spiritual growth within the community. The Rev. Dar Berkenpas says "Spiritual Enhancement is important to the development of the whole individual - the physical, spiritual, psychological and emotional aspects are all interrelated. Into the twenty first century, as human beings discover the dependency on the environment, it will be essential that the spiritual side of the human being is highly developed in order for the natural creative order of the earth to be maintained.

Rev. Berkenpas continues "Dialogue between Christian denominations and other world religions is to be encouraged - the survival of the earth depends on it."

Dr. Kent Hunter, Director of the Church Growth Center in Indiana says, "I concur with your assumption that any planning like that which you are doing ought to include opportunities that encourage individual and collective spiritual growth within the community. Without moral and religious fiber, a city is a concentration of life without depth, a seedbed for meaningless existence, and a greenhouse of frustration and deterioration."

In many communities Interfaith Volunteer Caregivers have proven to be a major resource for older chronically ill or disabled family members or friends.

•AARP's "Our Parents, Our Children, Ourselves," "Making Wise Decisions," "Home Is Where the Care Is," and the NCCW "Respite" video are available.# 16

•How to get Churches and Synagogues involved in services to Seniors. # 17

## 1. Churches

Churches will be encouraged to make every effort through good stewardship practices to lease share facilities such as buildings and parking lots with businesses and other denominations whenever possible. The churches will lease space from the UNI-CITI

Corporation within the UNI-CITI CENTRE or outer service park area.

Alan Burlison says, individuals do not perceive spiritual matters to the same degree. To some, it may be laissez-faire, while to others it is a matter of special concern. To some, the manner and place of worship will be extremely important and to others, it may well be a big deal about nothing. The concept of UNI use worship, style and process, is conceptually idealistic. The ideals of religious liberty must be protected, provided for, and even encouraged, for the mental well being of the individual. To this extent, it will be necessary to provide opportunity for unique and dedicated facilities for these interests. While this may seem wasteful to the casual observer, it is a small price to pay for development of the total individual. This situation is similar to rental or lease of space at hotels or convention centers.

Dr. Kent Hunter states that "Locating the church in close connection with the outer park service area has a good theological base so that recreation can become re-creation like they intended it. While many in our society consider leisure and worship, recreation and church to be conflicting opportunities, theologically they are as close as the day of rest--instituted by God himself."

Dr. Hunter continues "The idea of leasing shared facilities is a good one. With the cost of buildings, the richest community must wrestle with priorities for ministry that involves people while recognizing the importance of quality space for interactive fellowship, worship, and education."

Dr. Hunter says "Sharing with other denominations may be difficult. This may be an issue of self-centeredness or it may be connected to the fact that people value what they own and the related issue that states, that land has great meaning for personal and group identity. This would be the Old Testament promised land."

## 2. Media (Spiritual)

The closed circuit cable system will be available for spiritual enhancement. Other informational media such as print, radio and computer access will be available.

•Communications Systems **#18**

## C. EDUCATIONAL AND MIND DEVELOPMENT

Because "we are what we know," UNISONIA is the ultimate opportunity to develop the minds of all uni-citizens. Life for all is constantly an education toward greater fulfillment mentally as well as remunerative monetarily, with the knowledge that "people won't care how much you know until they know how much you care." These two statements appear to conflict but are intended to show the need for a caring attitude in order to have a sound basis for knowledge development.

> *"We don't know who we are until we see what we can do."*
> ~ **Martha Grimes**

•A great effort and emphasis will constantly be made to help all students "learn how to learn" **#19**

George Tash, owner of a small plumbing-parts company in Moorpark, CA., doesn't mind that his 13-year old son, Adam, accompanies him to work every day. In fact, he insists on it. That's because Adam attends school on the premises of his father's company, G.T. Water Products.

Tash's 24 year-old company is housed in a converted warehouse in the industrial district of Moorpark, near Los Angeles. The firm has 30 employees and annual sales of $3.5 million.

PHOTO: © BART BARTHOLOMEW

The school on his company's premises for his employee's children makes the workplace "more of a family affair," says owner George Tash, left. He and teacher Brian Kearsey check students' progress.

The school that Adam and 15 other children of company employees attend is financed entirely by the company and is in an enclosed section of the firm's warehouse.

A whole-life-long learning approach with free access to mind development, challenging everyone to broaden their understanding of themselves, others, and the world around them is the intent of UNISONIA.

# LOESCH

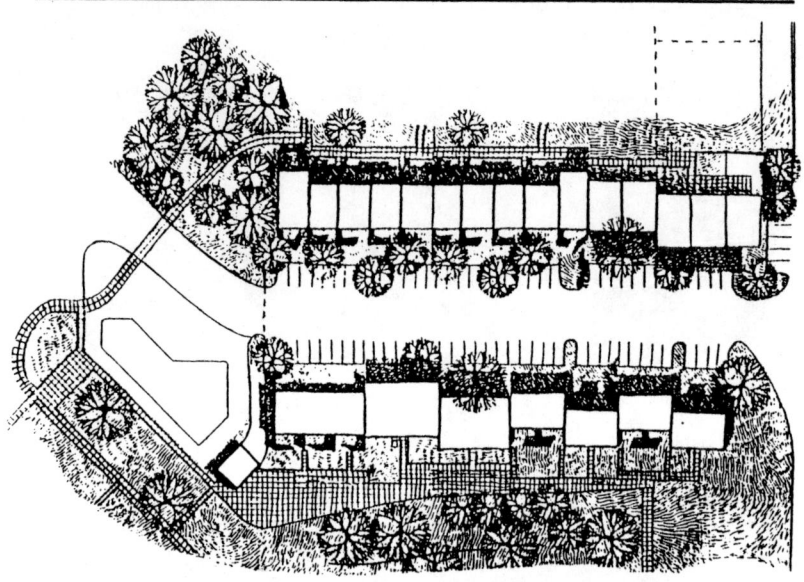

Garden apartments are shown on top of picture. Activity Center including convenience store, laundromat, meeting rooms, health center, swimming pool as well as other amenities are located in each UNI-PARK.

Each Uni-Park has a growth center for general use by all ages. The Uni-Quad Cluster plan could place a Learning Center within the Uni-Quad Park where it would be central for the whole Uni-Quad, instead of using the individual Uni-Park Growth Centers.

Nuclear Age Education is included in the curriculum of UNISONIA.

What is Nuclear Age Education?

* Helping teachers promote dialogue about controversial issues in ways that balance a questioning attitude and a search for common ground.

* Helping students develop new perspectives on issues such as global interdependence, security in the nuclear age, U.S.-World relations, and conflict resolution.

* Fostering mutual respect and understanding among people with diverse opinions and different cultural backgrounds.

*"Democracy without morality is impossible."*
*~Jack Kemp*

* Encouraging initiative, service, and a sense of community.

*"A child without hope, is a child without a future."*
*~Anonymous*

* Preparing students to be participating citizens in a democracy.

* Creating a vision of the future that nourishes hope.

•Educators for Social Responsibility, Sponsor; and the Center for Teaching Peace **#20**

## 1. Preschool (Day Care)

Preschool services will be located within each growth center and also, if market dictates, in the UNI-CITI CENTRE. These areas will offer many creative learning opportunities to experience the beginnings of a fulfilled life, maintained by a professional manager with oversight and guidance of the Homeowners Association.

The preschool services may be coordinated with volunteers of retirement/intermediate care center areas.

The preschool facilitators will provide your child with a variety of learning activities, including group and individual instruction.

For preschoolers, ages 2-5, there is a monthly thematic curriculum, with emphasis on readiness activities.

Learning for Living, the unique Montessori-type preschool program includes: Practical Life Sensorial, Language Arts and Mathematics. Individual task completion is emphasized.

*"Cherishing children is the mark of a civilized society."*

~ **Joan Ganz Cooney**

All centers feature a computer center. Specially selected software ranges from basic preschool language and math readiness to elementary age programming.

For elementary school children, well-designed programs provide a vital group during, before-and after-school time.

Centers also offer special developmental programs for infants and toddlers.

•The goal is to enable your child to have a positive self-concept and to know success from the beginning offering

•a true learning experience for your child. **#21** La Petite **#22** Preschool Intergenerational Programs **#23**

## 2. Elementary

School children from grades one to six will also be located at the Growth Centers operated by each UNI-PARK Association. These school facilities will be tied into the home computer center in all homes in the UNI-CITI.

> *"If a child lives with approval, he learns to like himself.,"*
>
> ~ **Dorothy Law Nolte**

In Unisonian schools, emphasis is placed on four areas: care of self and the environment, sensory and motor education, writing and reading, and premath skills.

Children may be enrolled as early as infancy and may attend up through high school.

Teachers attend training programs to prepare them for their work. Since self-motivation and self-education by the student is a key component of the schooling method, teachers trained for conventional elementary teaching must rethink megatrends approach to the classroom. The teacher/observer is trained to set up specific learning environments consisting of games and materials that encourage motor-skill development, sensory learning, and acquisition of vocabulary.

Classrooms often seem surprisingly quiet compared with other nursery schools as a result of the clearly established patterns followed by the children on their own. Classes place emphasis on the children's tasks and do

> *"Children are likely to live up to what you believe of them."*
>
> ~ **Lady Bird Johnson**

not encourage the same kind of free play and fantasy often found in other types of nursery schools. Children attend to their "work," and the teacher remains in the background.

This system of education is both a philosophy of child growth and a rationale for guiding such growth. It is based on the child's developmental needs for freedom and a carefully prepared environment which guarantees exposure to materials and experiences through which to develop intelligence as well as physical and psychological abilities. It is designed to take full advantage of the self-motivation and unique ability of young children to develop their own capabilities. Children need adults to expose them to the possibilities of their lives, but the children themselves must direct their responses to those possibilities.

Key premises of this education method are:

1. Children are to be respected as different from adults, and as individuals who differ from each other.

2. Children possess unusual sensitivity and mental powers for absorbing and learning from their environment that are unlike those of the adults both in quantity and capacity.

3. The most important years of growth are the first six years of life when unconscious learning is gradually brought to the conscious level.

4. Children have a deep love and need for purposeful work. The child works, however, not as an adult for profit and completion of a job, but for sake of the activity itself. It is this activity which accomplishes the most important goal for the child: the development of his or her mental, physical, and psychological powers.

## Is it for all children?

This system has been used successfully with children between ages two and a half and eighteen from all socio-economic levels, representing those in regular classes as well as the gifted, the retarded, the emotionally disturbed, and the physically handicapped. Because of its individual approach, it is uniquely suited to public education, where children of many backgrounds are grouped together. It is also appropriate for classes in which the student-teacher ratio is high because children learn at an early age to work independently.

> *"What we want to see is the child in pursuit of knowledge, not knowledge in pursuit of the child.*
>
> ~ **George Bernard Shaw**

## Is it oriented to a particular religion?

It is not associated with a particular religious persuasion.

Groups have sponsored schools representing non-sectarian interests as well as Catholic, Jewish, Protestant, and Hindu faiths.

## Is the child free to do what he chooses in the classroom?

The child is free to move about the classroom at will, to talk to other children, to work with any equipment he or she understands, or to ask the teacher to introduce new material to him or her. The child is not free to disturb other children at work or to abuse the equipment that is so important to each child's development.

## What does the teacher do?

The teacher is working with individual children, introducing materials and giving guidance where needed. A primary task is careful observation of each child to determine his or her needs and to gain the knowledge needed in preparing the environment to aid each child's growth. The method of teaching is indirect in that it neither imposes upon the child as in direct teaching, nor abandons the child as in a non-directive, permissive approach. Rather, the teacher is constantly alert to the direction in which the child has indicated he or she wishes to go, and actively works to help the child achieve his or her goals.

*Imagination*
*A mind once stretched by a new idea never regains its original dimensions.*

~ **Celebrating Excellence**
**Lombard, IL**

**What does it do for the child?**

Observers of children taught under this system have described them as having developed self-discipline, self-knowledge, and

independence, as well as enthusiasm for learning, an organized approach to problem-solving, and academic skills. #24

## 3. Secondary

Grades seven through twelve are housed in the UNI- CITI CENTRE which will provide opportunities to become directly involved in business experience as well as being involved in other varied services within the centre.

The same attitudes of self-motivation and self education by the student continues to be key components of the teaching methods through secondary, post high school, vocational, and beyond. Creative ways of motivating such actions are encouraging.

## Learning Banks Invest in Students

A learning bank is a cooperative program in Fargo and West Fargo, North Dakota and Moorhead, Minnesota that, according to Phil Matthews, Business Columnist of The Fargo Forum, aims to make better use of all the public schools through a blending of educational resources.

One of The Learning Bank,s projects is a career exploration program for high school students which is an opportunity for young people to spend some time working or observing in a job or profession.

Jacqueline Brodshaug of Fargo, director of the Learning Bank says, "The business community is one of the resources of the schools, as well as the recipient of what the schools produce."

PHOTO : FRANK ZAGARINO—BLACK STAR

First-grade teacher Karen Bourgmann reads to a class at the American Bankers satellite school; the facility has become an inducement in recruiting workers.

In the Career Bank program, the people in various businesses and occupations of the community are being asked to open their doors to the high school students and their career planning.

"If people who are active in business or in the professions are willing to share in this career exploration, the students will gain by having some new insights in that occupation," she said.

Brodschaug emphasized the financial importance of cooperation in the community in the Learning Bank programs.

She states, "As our resources in all the schools become more limited under tight budget controls, there are ways the community resources can be extended and be made better use of. This blending of the resources can mean two important achievements.

You can offer more educational opportunities for your students, and you can save dollars for the taxpayer."

Charles Bailly is a Fargo businessman who has been a strong supporter of the Learning Bank as well as other innovations in education.

"The Career Bank is an attempt to let the students learn more about the careers that are available to them," he said. "This will be done by using people in business, in industry and in the professions as first-hand resources."

The Learning Bank conducted a study last year to learn what the students felt they needed for a fuller educational experience. One of the major requests was for more opportunities in career exploration.

"Students are being taken seriously," Brodshaug said. "Some want to be prepared for an occupation or a job upon graduation from high school. All students do not go on to college."

•Learning Bank Information **#25**
•Where There Is A Will There Is An A **#26**


**In Tokyo, Industry and Academic Peer into a Common Future** - according to Harlan Cleveland of the Minneapolis Star Tribune.

The keynote speakers uttering the following Japanese heresies were not wild-eyed radicals. They were sober and reflective government officials. The occasion was a meeting in Tokyo of University presidents and other educators from Asia, Europe, Latin America, and North America, to talk about how corporations and higher education, can and should work together worldwide.

"Japan is about to enter the information-intensive society."

"We need to learn how to create creativity, and learn when it ripens. A chess grandmaster, or a great violinist, may show up as a five-year-old. But Einstein's genius was not obvious until he was in junior high school."

"Advanced education is no longer just for the upper classes."

A college education is indispensable for a good job."

"A pragmatic meritocracy is gaining ground." "Female students can no longer be sidetracked into junior colleges."

"At first we need to 'learn from the west.' So imparting knowledge was the thing to do. But now, Japan must generate its own creative thinking. Large lectures need to be replaced by small classes."

"We used to emphasize mass production. But now we think it is most important to develop the individual."

An educated person "should have the special knowledge to dig a deep hole to start with. But vertical knowledge is not enough. The premium now is on horizontal knowledge, the capacity to integrate."

The future will be characterized by "complexity, mobility, rapid change, uncertainty, and vulnerability." "What is needed is education for flexibility, for originality."

The Megatrends in higher education are strikingly similar in Japan, Europe and the United States. Some insights from the Tokyo conference: quantitative growth is due to slacken, even though equal access is not yet achieved, as the supply of 18-year-olds shrinks. (In Japan, 18-year-olds will peak at 2.05 million in 1992 and dwindle to 1.35 million by 2005. The size of Japanese higher education is expected to decline by one-third in those thirteen years. In the richer parts of the world, higher educators will be focusing ever more on the qualities of what students get.

> *"The hours that make us happy make us wise."*
>
> ~ **John Mansfield**

Lifelong education is the wave of the future: Mixing his metaphors, one expert said "the center of gravity is moving up the age ladder." For universities that raise their sights beyond the 18-25 age cohort, the life long markets will offset the sagging enrollments of young students. But that will require a wholesale reform of "continuing education," which is still a second-class citizen in nearly all universities. It will no longer be good enough to deliver to 40-year-olds and 60-year-olds, at convenient times and places, coursework designed for 20-year-olds.

The learning of "facts" is giving way to "learning how to learn." "What is learned in college is obsolete after a year or so," said a Japanese industrialist, explaining why corporations have mounted such large schools and colleges of their own. (Next to me, an expert muttered a startling statistic: "In the United States, in-house corporate education now overmatches the nationwide cost of public elementary and secondary schools.")

"Careers" will no longer be stable and predictable; "job security" is becoming an oxymoron. Scientific discovery and technological innovation keep flushing out of the labor force whatever work can be done better by machines, while creating even more opportunities for work that people can do better -- if they are "educated for flexibility."

**What should be "higher" about higher education?**

When they come together at a meeting such as this, the leaders of business, government and education reach a ready consensus: The fastest growing need in "advanced" learning is for people who can fuse the specialized expertise of others in systems and organizations that address the megaproblems of our time.

Out in the real world beyond academy, everyone knows that the most puzzling and most important problems are interdepartmental, interdisciplinary, interprofessional, and international. Integrative minds are at a premium. Japan, says a Japanese educator, needs above all "open-minded" individuals who can see many points of view."

In these circumstances, what earthly sense does it make that the Ph.D., the highest credential provided by universities in every country, is still earned for pursuing the narrowest courses of study?

**4. Adult (Pre-Retirement)**

Every opportunity will be

*"Experimenting is the secret of eternal youth."*
*~Author Unknown*

pursued to make all experiences whether during work or leisure times enjoyable, fulfilling and beneficial to all individuals, opening their world to creative growth and involvement in contact with UNISONIA.

## 5. Adult (Post Retirement)

Encouragement and guidance for retired individuals to take advantage of all possible positive reinforcers will be actively provided.

In home education TV hookups with the central educational facility will carry programming of special interest to post-retirement adults.

Pre-retirement and post-retirement adults will be kept abreast of intergenerational developments within the Uni-Citi.

Recent literature on aging indicates that one of the most important tasks of aging is "reminiscence." It is important both for therapeutic reasons and as a living legacy to family. Participants learn how to effectively evoke memories, stories, and creative expression through techniques designed to tap key experiences. Emphasis is on oral history gathering through sound tapes and videotapes as well as professionally written journals. Sponsored by Horwich/Kaplan Jewish Community Center.

Another program known as "Yesteryear" provides volunteer managers/staff with a model of a rural intergenerational program designed for personal interaction between RSVP senior volunteers and grade school students. #27

Another videotape program involves seniors and their families with family-made videotapes which offer an additional way for families and nursing home residents to communicate. Watching the tapes appears to connect the resident on an emotional level with his or her family. The experience also has a positive impact on family members and staff. # 28
•See also # 29

ILLUSTRATIONS BY HUNT ASSOCIATES/STEVE SCHLENKER

## Senior Housing

A wide chasm often exists between homebound older adults and 14-16 year old adolescents. The Hands Helping Hands program forges links between young and old. Young adults learn work and employment skills and the homebound older adults over-come their distrust and fear of the youth. The learning translates into unique and special time together.

•Hands Helping Hands information. **# 30**

In order to make these connections happen, home environments must be appropriate. Some housing options available for seniors in UNISONIA are presented on the following pages.

Information about senior housing pertaining to Uni-Park/Uni-Cities is available in a summary of information provided by the AARP in a booklet "Housing Options for Older Americans." **#31**

Most older people want to stay put. They tell us they are reluctant to give up their homes of many years because they are comfortable in the neighborhood and secure in the knowledge that they are near familiar stores and close friends.

However, 30 percent of older persons do move sometime after their 65th birthday. Yet only 3 percent purchase or rent homes, and only about 4 percent move out of the state in which they lived the day they reached sixty-five. For those who want to stay put and for those who are thinking of moving, the following material explains some of the housing and living arrangements to consider. Some ideas and alternatives are new; some are still in the developing phase.

For many years, the American Association of Retired Persons (AARP) has studied the housing needs of older Americans and monitored developments in housing practices and policies.

Following are some of the most pertinent housing methods for senior Uni-Citizens.


**Homes and Apartments**

Housing is not just a roof over your head. It is a life style - your life style. So take a good look at yourself first; it will then be easier to make decisions about the kind of living arrangements best for you. The time to give careful thought to the growing number of housing choices is before an emergency or crisis forces you into a decision.

You will not only need to choose the right location for your new home, but you will need to decide what type of housing best meets your needs. For many older persons, home ownership is an aspiration that has been pursued and accomplished. Ownership provides a sense of satisfaction and permanence that some find lacking in rental arrangements. Moreover, the rising market value of residential property has made home ownership a good investment.

ILLUSTRATIONS BY HUNT ASSOCIATES/STEVE SCHLENKER

Garden homes located across from the Activity Center in each UNI-PARK

Home Ownership: No federal home ownership program focuses specifically on the elderly, but older persons can get help from a variety of federal programs aimed at encouraging home ownership. HUD, for example, runs mortgage insurance programs designed to promote ownership among financially qualified buyers of condominiums and cooperative units and to stimulate development of this kind of housing by qualified sponsors under HUD Sections 234 and 213. HUD also runs mortgage insurance and interest subsidy programs to encourage the building and financing of housing for low and moderate income home buyers under Section 235. Information on these programs is available from HUD Area Offices.

Veterans Administration: The Veterans Administration has a number of programs to assist veterans as well as spouses of persons who have died as a result of military service. VA home loan guarantees, providing protection against default on the loan, were originally a one-time benefit. In 1978, however, Congress revised the legislation to allow a veteran who has satisfied the obligations of a previous VA loan to be eligible for a new home loan guarantee, which generally involves single family homes. Nevertheless, it is possible for a qualifying veteran to purchase a condominium or cooperative unit with this guarantee or for two or more eligible veterans to join together to buy a multi-family building.

Under certain conditions, the VA can also make home loans directly to veterans. Such loans are available particularly in areas that the VA has designated as credit shortage areas.

The VA also runs a grant program designed for the special needs of veterans with service-connected disabilities. This program helps veterans to buy or remodel a home in order to provide it with the special equipment disabled veterans may need for independent living. Information about loan limits, terms, eligibility criteria, and application procedures is available at state or local VA offices.

## Echo Housing

Some older persons have thought about living with their children or other members of the family and perhaps have rejected the idea because they felt they would lose their independence or become a burden. One new solution to this dilemma is ECHO housing (Elder Cottage Housing Opportunity). An ECHO house is a separate, self-contained unit designed for temporary installation in the side or backyard of an adult child's home. It is a concept that permits closeness without sacrificing self-reliance.

The idea originated in Australia under the name of "granny flats." The Victoria Ministry of Housing installs and rents the units and then removes them when they are no longer needed.

A few manufacturers in this country are beginning to make ECHO homes that cost about $14,000 to $20,000. Because the homes are both removable and reusable, they're generally produced as manufactured housing.

Family Benefits: The benefits of ECHO housing can be substantial. For example, Frederick County, Maryland permits ECHO units as special exceptions to single-family zoning in certain districts. People who have taken advantage of the option are eloquent advocates of the idea. A widow who moved into an ECHO unit a few feet from her daughter's house says her new home allows her to make ends meet. Her daughter adds, "All of us were worried about mother being by herself. Now that she doesn't have to keep up her big house, she is free to do things she has never been able to do before."

## Home-Matching Programs

Cluster housing approaches would fulfill needs spoken of in ECHO housing above.

Some old and traditional ways of solving housing problems are gaining new support among legislators, community leaders and the public. One example is the growing number of shared housing match-up programs in which would-be home or apartment sharers are introduced to home or apartment seekers.

These arrangements are becoming more common thanks to individual initiative and public or private agencies that specialize in matching services. Participants include older people, one-parent families, moderate or low-income singles, students, and the divorced or widowed. Some agencies also offer their services to people with mental or physical disabilities.

Programs In Action: In Los Angeles, former school teacher Janet Witkin organized a group of volunteers, rented a storefront office and founded a nonprofit home-matching service called Housing Alternatives for Seniors.

To date, the service has found sharing arrangements for more than 600 older people. Donations and a modest federal grant help defray the program's cost. Applicants complete a questionnaire about attitudes concerning such things as smoking, hobbies, diets, and overnight guests.

Older people are learning that two or three can live more cheaply than one person alone. "Many of them have found that living with an older housemate is easier than moving in with their grown children." Wittkin said.

In Montgomery County, Maryland, Operation Match offers a clearinghouse service to link people offering living space with people seeking housing. It began as a service for older people, but the organizers soon learned that demand for shared housing

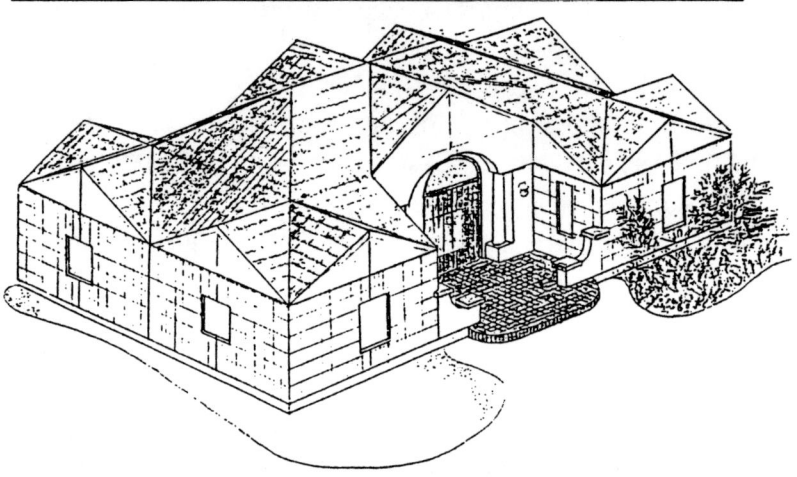

The LOESCH DESIGNED PANULAR HOUSE is engineered to be used as an alternative affordable housing method.

was not limited to any single age group. The program now includes single parents, recently widowed persons, people in the midst of divorce or separation, and handicapped persons. Older people comprise fewer than 50 percent of the clientele.

Home-matching services are forming in various places around the country. However, they still aren't keeping pace with the potential demand. Communities can help by organizing services to bring people together to satisfy their housing needs. The results can be better communities, with more available and affordable housing, and better lives for many people.


## Shared Housing

Shared housing is another new option being explored by individuals, communities and the government as a way to provide adequate, affordable housing for older people. In this scheme, two or more unrelated individuals share the common areas of a house, while all have their own private space. Usually, the house is owned by a public or private agency rather than by any one resident.


## Proven Space Use Designs

Following are several very practical home layouts shown in Better Homes and Gardens Magazine **# 32**

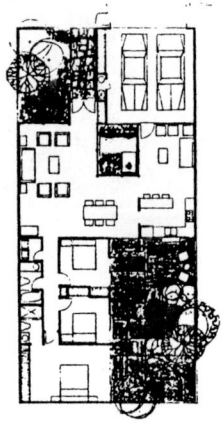

Although this garden town-house plan actually connects homes. The way it's done leads you to forget you have nearby neighbors. The small front yard is secluded and the rear garden is walled in for complete privacy. An atrium brings a touch of the outdoors into the middle of each living area. The bedroom wing juts rearward and opens all three room to light, view, and air in a way today's typical houses in this price range don't even attempt.

# UNISONIA

BETTER HOMES AND GARDENS

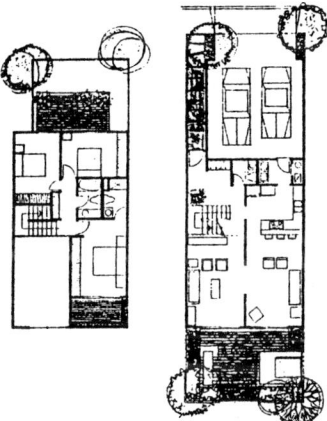

Compact convenience best describes this two-story town house plan. Downstairs, the front entry is spacious enough to welcome a whole group of guests. Access to the family cars couldn't be more direct. The living room stretches two stories high and borrows space from the open stairway (it thus seems much larger than its actual size). Upstairs, the three bedrooms have generous storage, and all three open to secluded, upper level decks.

BETTER HOMES AND GARDENS, AUGUST, 1970

55

BETTER HOMES AND GARDENS

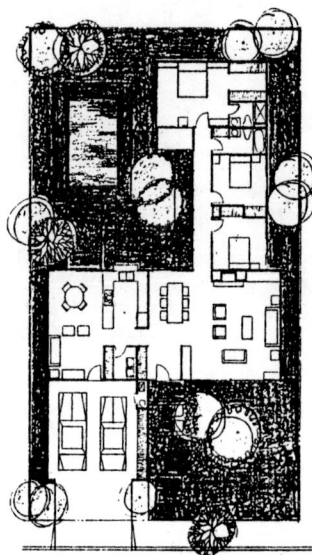

This detailed plan shows what you should expect from both house and lot in

a four-per-acre situation. The front yard is small and the driveway short - two factors which cut summer and winter work to a minimum. The rest of the house is open and private at the same time; no room is dark and dreary, and all of the views are concentrated. Houses built on land planned this efficiently offer plenty of opportunity for variety, because the sites are large enough to allow for changes in the shape size of homes.

BETTER HOMES AND GARDENS

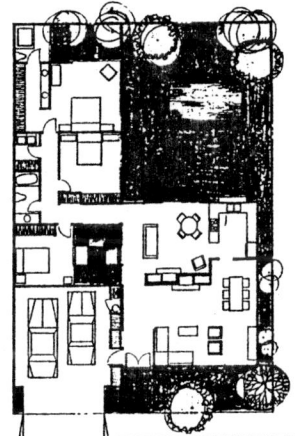

A great plan for any narrow city lot situation, this neatly zones the living area away from the quiet bedrooms. Living and dining are up front, separated from the action of the kitchen and family room. The happenings there are only a step away from the outside, and the swimming pool proves that you don't really need an estate. One bedroom gets its light and view from the atrium; the other two share the family room's view of the backyard. The master bath-dressing area makes the best possible use of the space there, and the bathing compartment opens to the outside for access to and from the pool.

*"If we apply the theory of ecology to urban design, we can integrate the pieces to create a whole, nurturing environment.*

*If we reweave the pieces so that women, men, nature, spirit, public, private are all equally valued, they would all be sacred and balance into one whole, with no part removed or left out.*

*We need to blur the separations between men and women, urban and natural, between public and private.*

*We need to bring the attributes of each to the other, and then every element of our communities would have inherent value and also contribute to ecological balance.*

*We would then attain both physical and cultural balance."*

Julia Walton, from "Community and the New Urban Village"

# PART II
## ENVIRONMENTAL AND LAND USE

The attitude of UNISONIA is one of conservation and experimentation of practices which benefit both Uni-Citizens and the Environment. UNISONIA is a minimum atrophy approach with a transitional step into a non-entropy objective. Proper natural land enhancement practices will put back into the soil the nutrients taken out. Such practice will be encouraged both within UNISONIAN communities and in surrounding agricultural endeavors.

•*Mother Earth News* and others **# 32**


## A.  RESOURCE MANAGEMENT

Resources creatively managed can provide a multitude of benefits monetarily, recreationally, agriculturally, and aesthetically.

Uni-Citizens will become knowledgeable of permacultural methods as defined by Wes Jackson  and of other agricultural and non-agricultural  resources management techniques through print, media and other research.

## 1. Water

Water will always be held in high regard. Special care in properly using this valuable resource to eliminate unnecessary processing, contamination and handling will make more and better economic use of less water. Every known practical precaution to eliminate danger from such health hazards as chlorine from drinking will be taken. Central deionization, ozoneation, or bacteriostatic, granular activated carbon microorganism water treatment systems may be provided for entire complex and/or separate systems for each Uni-Park.

**"Use of Ozone Yields Drinking Water Free of Bacteria, Chlorine After Taste, "**- was a headline in Newark Star-Ledger Special Report, by Gordon Bishop in May 1988.

Ozone, a key ingredient in creating suffocating smog, as well as a life protecting shield against deadly radiation is now being hailed as the best way of attacking bacteria in drinking water supplies. Ozone, a form of oxygen, can either harm or improve life on earth, depending on how it is used. As a substitute for chlorine, ozone can kill bacteria without the side effects caused by chlorine, including cancerous diseases and hardening of the arteries.

About 30 of the nation's 60,000 water companies, including the Hackensack, New Jersey, Water Co., have turned to ozone to destroy bacteria and viruses in their water treatment plants. Unlike chlorine, a deadly gas, ozone does not spin off such cancer-causing "precursors" as trihalomethanes or chloroform. Water, "after ozone does its job" changes back to normal, life-sustaining oxygen, within 30 minutes. For that miraculous reason, Hackensack Water will be treating its drinkable supplies with ozone. "Consumers will notice obvious improvements at the tap," said Thomas McKeon, Vice-President of Operations at Hackensack Water, the state's largest purveyor, with nearly a million consumers. McKeon goes on to state, "Ozone is an effective bacteriacide and inactivates viruses better than chlorine and it's cheaper, too, in the overall treatment process." The company expects to save $10 million in construction costs. An additional savings of $25 million will be realized in operations over the life of the $65 million, 220 million gallon-per-day treatment plant. The facility will be the second largest in the U. S.

International Ozonation Association publications:

- Ozonation Manual For Water and Wastewater Treatment Proceedings of Ozone World Congress
- Applications of Ozone in Water Treatment
- Ozonation - Environmental Impact and Benefit
- Ozone and Biology
- International Ozone Symposium - Wasser Berlin 1985
- Ozone and Ultra-Violet water treatment
- Analytical Aspects of Ozone Ground Water Quality Protection
- Rural Ground Water Contamination
- Toxic Contamination in Large Lakes
- Aquatic Applications of Ozone
- Forum on Ozone Disinfection
- Design and Operation of Ozone Systems for Drinking Water Plants

•Ozonation **# 33**
•IOA Pan American Committee, Information **# 34**
•Bacteriostatic Granular Activated carbon water filtration **# 35**

## a. Domestic Potable

Uni-citizens will make use of control-flow shower heads and other automatic shut off valves where water waste takes place. The wisdom of such conservation is understood and appreciated.

The Concept - All tank type heaters work on the storage principle. They STORE heated water - waiting for use. This cost's money (your money!). The tank constantly cycles on and off - continuously, twenty-four hours a day - day in and day out - even when the owner is away on vacation.

Instant water heating systems are based upon the DEMAND PRINCIPLE. They do not store so much as a single drop of heated water. Instead, when a faucet is opened, they sense need and turn on automatically to make hot water instantly - and continuously - for as long as needed. As an added benefit - these tankless systems simply cannot run out of hot water - because they do not store hot water - they produce it - ON DEMAND.

This basic difference in engineering approach (Storage vs. Demand) is responsible for the wonderful savings unit owners are enjoying right now. Energy costs continue to rise. Predictions are that this steady trend will continue. Whether you heat hot water by gas or electricity, there is an instant unit that can be attached to your present system right now.

The U.S. Dept. of Energy has calculated average daily hot water usage for a family of four to be 64.3 gallons. On a yearly basis, this equals 23,470 gallons of hot water. Throughout most of the world energy has always been relatively costly. Now, high energy prices have come to America, too - with them, the need to conserve. Since the ordinary storage-type hot water heater is probably THE single most costly-to-operate "appliance" in the average home, conservation (and money saving, too) could begin meaningfully right at the old-fashioned tank. Of course, every drop of hot water you DO NOT USE will save money. You can realize savings immediately by simply using less. Water restrictors placed on shower heads and faucets are good energy, water and money savers, too. But, the TANKLESS SYSTEMS presented in these pages go beyond basic conservation by offering a NEW SOLUTION TO HOT WATER HEATING. This easy-to-understand new concept (Demand rather than Storage) works!

Long Life is an Added Bonus - The Demand System, for example, is basically NOT SUBJECT TO LEAKS - as is a tank. It should not "lime up" to the same extent either.

Storage tanks constantly radiate heat contained in the stored water - through tank walls and into crawl space or attic - winter or summer - day and night. A U.S. Government agency study reveals that the average household uses hot water a total of perhaps one-and-a-half hours a day. For this convenience, tanks must STAND BY WITH HEATED WATER - constantly. Since even the newer, more efficient tank insulations cannot be 100% efficient and thus cannot contain all the stored heat, this cycle of heating and cooling goes on indefinitely--even when the owner is away for a day--or a week (unless, of course, the heater is completely shut off). Engineers call this "stand by loss" -- and it is inherent in the DESIGN CONCEPT OF ALL storage systems.  The booster unit may be used for SOLAR HOT WATER HEATING

## Installations

An automatic thermostat built into the booster unit will add additional heat ONLY when the Solar System needs boosting. On cloudy, winter days when the Solar System needs help, the booster unit senses both the demand for water and the need for additional capacity. Then it cuts in automatically to supply JUST THE PRECISE AMOUNT OF ADDITIONAL HEAT YOU REQUIRE.

•Slow and self closing faucets and low flow showerheads. # 36
•Instant Water Heating Systems. # 37

## b.  Environmental

Water will be used agriculturally through drip irrigation and in hydroponics, primarily watering only areas intended to be watered.  Drip irrigation eliminates evaporation to a great degree. Canals, lakes and fountains will use a substantial amount of unprocessed water.  Lakes and canals will be lined in order to keep from losing water to seepage whenever beneficially appropriate. However, evaporation will take place generally and through aeration from waterfalls and fountains.

## WATERFALL CONFIGURATIONS

Rugged step-falls    Overhanging falls    Slip falls

Two-story falls              Curtain falls

Regular step-falls              Ribbon falls

From "A Touch of Japanese for Your Garden."

## 2. Waste Resources

What in most instances is considered waste and of no value can be profitably processed and provide not only financial value from sale of materials but also employment value.

A patented system specifically designed to process municipal refuse is now available. In one hour of operation, each system can convert 25 tons of unsorted refuse into a homogeneous, relatively dry, odorless, fluff. The system consists of a feed conveyor, rotating centrifugal mill, and off load conveyor. The rotating mill includes a rough grind section, followed by increasingly finer communition sections. In each section, wastes are ground and pulverized by the centrifugal action. The rate of flow of material is controlled to achieve desired product consistency. Controlled air flow achieves drying and consistent processing of lighter fractions of the waste. This results in an odorless, manageable milled product which will then become a composite material in manufactured products. **#38**
•Paper shredding machine **#39**

Solid waste compost organizations use research being done by University of Minnesota scientists who are trying to answer basic questions about the potential for solid waste compost: Is there a market for it and how large is the market?

The answers could have a major impact in landfill abatement plans. Biodegradable material such as garbage and paper comprises a large part of solid waste. Composting this material and knowing how to use it could mean that less waste would need to be disposed of. Also, the Citi would have a homegrown substitute for the topsoil and soil amendments that some non-food industries buy now.

One aspect of the research, being conducted by soil and horticultural scientists at the University of Minnesota, is investigating the chemical, biological and physical properties of solid waste compost. Which nutrients and contaminants does solid waste compost contain and in what levels? How does the incorporation of solid waste compost affect soil microbes and the soil's physical properties?

The research has included plant growth studies with container-grown ornamentals and greenhouse grown bedding plants. In addition, the effects of applying solid waste compost to roadsides are being studied in small test plots.

In another part of the study, potential users of solid waste compost are golf course superintendents, nurserymen, landscape contractors, cemetery maintenance personnel, and others.

**Biomass Refinery**

An integrated municipal solid waste processing facility, the Biomass Refinery is designed to dispose of municipal solid waste ("MSW").

The facility was engineered to utilize approximately 90% of the incoming MSW volume to manufacture valuable commercial products for sale, principally fuel ethanol, with the remaining 10% residue being principally "sterilized dirt," resulting in major environmental benefits to communities. Both the stack gases and the liquid waste streams will be treated for pollution control, resulting in little or no pollution discharge from the facility.

Hazardous waste can be molecularly modified to a benign product by a high degree of heat. PCB's to $2172^0$ F. and organic contamination such as gasoline contaminated dirt at $1386^0$ F. Burners are available at $3982^0$ F. **# 40**

Additionally, the facility is designed to dispose of scrap tires, utilizing them as a partial energy source in the facility's cogeneration unit, where steam and electricity will be generated making the facility nearly energy self sufficient. All the equipment for the facility is standardized and can be ordered "off the shelf" in packaged operating units.

The Company believes its new chemical technology (the Biomass Process) is unique in the world today, providing the "high-tech" solution to economically process MSW into valuable chemicals, resulting in an environmentally acceptable disposal method for MSW and the solution to the present nationwide MSW dilemma created by landfilling and incineration of MSW.

No burning of the MSW takes place in a Biomass Refinery, thus no toxic ash is created.

"The Biomass Process could have worldwide impact," stated Company spokesman Alan Neves, who has been in charge of developing the technology for the Company during the past ten years. "It is environmentally safe, because we don't burn MSW and we don't bury it; we process it chemically in a way that is environmentally benign producing no toxic air or water emissions."

The principal commercial product from a Biomass Refinery is fuel ethanol, which is used to raise octane ratings in unleaded gasoline, and reportedly, can lower pollutants from automobiles. Ethanol is also widely used in the pharmaceutical and cosmetic industries. For municipalities, though, reducing the volume of materials that need to be landfilled is the most important consideration at this time.

The Company is optimistic about the construction of future Biomass Refineries in the United States because of the developing social conscience in America to find an environmentally acceptable way to dispose of MSW and other waste materials. The Company believes that the Biomass Process is an environmentally acceptable way to dispose of MSW and could create an immediate demand for Biomass Refineries worldwide. This type of approach is appropriate for use in UNI-Citi SOLID WASTE PROGRAMS. Biomass Refinery Information **#41**

## a. Recyclables

Water entering the household will be potable drinking water for use in many ways. However, clothes washing and bathing water will be filtered and recycled for use in flushing effluent from a 2-4 quart flush toilet, thereby saving many gallons of water per family unit per day. Four toilet flushes per person per day per citi of 10,000 is 40,000 flushes. Three and a half gallons per 40,000 flushes equals 140,000 gallons per day. Two quarts per 40,000 flushes equals 20,000 gallons per day equals 120,000 gallons saving per day or 43,800,000 gallons saving per year.

Flow reduction with minimum flush toilets (two quarts) means significant savings in sewage handling and treatment and original water treatment and processing.

Toilet flush water represents the largest single source of waste that enters disposal treatment system...as much as 90% of public use facilities and approximately 40% of residential wastewater. That's because conventional toilets use 3½ to 7 gallons of water per flush.

   Installation of air-assisted one-half gallon toilets translates directly into significant savings in sewage, construction and plumbing costs.

- •Flush Volume - This unit reduces flush volume as much as 90% by using only one-half gallon of water.

- •Flow Reduction - This flush unit contributes significantly to total reduction in water flow, approximately 40% for residences, and up to 90% for public use facilities.

   While the toilet represents a small percentage of total project costs, it is the largest water consuming, wastewater- producing element in the plumbing system.

   The unit will achieve major savings in sewage installation, water handling, wastewater treatment and land utilization costs.

- •By reducing water and sewer connection fees.

- •By allowing greater utilization of ground water supplies, and reducing ground water impacts.

The one-gallon toilet features:

Pressure flush - The incoming water fills the water tank, trapping air in the tank and compressing it to a pressure equal to that of the incoming water pressure. Once this water under pressure is released to the toilet bowl, it has sufficient jet action to clear the entire bowl of all waste and then replenish the bowl with water for the next usage. The lid must remain down for 20 seconds to complete the flush cycle. One gallon flush conserves 36% of household water according to the U.S. Department of the Interior study on "Flow Reduction and Treatment of Waste Water," and from the Ontario Ministry of the Environment study on the "Characteristics of Effluents."

Based on a 3 person, single-family household, if the 1-gallon Water Saver toilet is used in place of the 4-gallon flush toilet, the totals look like this:
= = = = = = = = = = = = = = = = = = = = = = = = = =

|  | 1 gal. | 4 gal. |
|---|---|---|
| @ 19.5 flushes per day: | | |
| Day | 19.5 gal. | 78.0 gal. |
| Month | 585.0 gal. | 2,340.0 gal. |
| Year | 7,020.0 gal. | 28,080.0 gal. |

2500 families 1 yr = 70,200,000 gal.

Using the 1-gallon Water Saver toilet in place of a 4-gallon flush toilet results in a 36% reduction in total water used.

Studies show that the effect on the sewage system is minimal with this reduction. Less than 2% of household sewage is solid material and therefore a reduction of 36% in water will not significantly affect the solids-to-liquids ratio and will not cause sewer blockage.

Effluent will be recycled together with other decomposable waste such as chipped and shredded wood, into useable compost after its methane producing value has been depleted. This composted material may be used for rental gardens, community tree plantings or for commercial resale. Other waste materials such as metal, glass, plastic, etc. will be separated by each household and placed in separate containers within two hundred

feet of each home unit. These waste materials will then be picked up for profitable recycling.
- Toilets  # 42
- Refuse Containers # 43
- Air Pressure System  # 44
- Methane Gas Collection System # 45

## b.  Effluent

Effluent, which is a large concern in any community, can through proper recycling become a profitable, positive value-producing substance.

The Pollution Control Plant for individual homes is a giant step into a clean new world -- out of the old fashioned world of the septic tank.

The plant is designed to serve homes beyond city sewers, anywhere. In just 24 hours, it reduces all household wastewater to a clear odorless liquid.

Developed as a replacement for the inefficient septic tank, the treatment plant uses the same central treatment plants. The plant simply adapts the process to a small compact underground installation sized to serve a single home.

Local health departments often insist on home aeration plants instead of septic tanks, especially where the water table is high or the soil has poor percolation.

The plant is self-contained, automatic, odorless. Designed for modern living, it easily handles wastewater from multiple-bath homes with all modern appliances - automatic laundries, dishwashers, garbage grinders. And yet it is a practical plant.

It does not cost a fortune to buy, operate or maintain. Most important, it requires little maintenance.

The treatment process - called extended aeration - is a speeded-up version of what happens in nature when a river tumbles through rapids and over waterfalls, purifying itself by capturing oxygen. The plant brings oxygen to the wastewater by an electrically operated aerator.

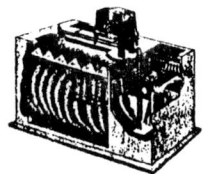

One Unit is located in each UNI-PARK

100,000 GPD JET Package Plant at Little Rock, Ark., subdivision

The clear liquid discharged by a plant is odorless and colorless. According to some scientific opinion, the high dissolved oxygen content in an aeration plant's oxygen-laden effluent actually contributes to the betterment of nearby streams, helping support aquatic life.

## A Central Treatment Plant in Miniature

The plant is constructed of rugged permanent concrete. Its design incorporates three separate compartments, each performing a specific function in the total purification process.

1. The primary treatment compartment receives the household wastewater and holds it long enough to allow solid matter to settle to the sludge layer at the tank's bottom. Organic solids are here broken down physically and biochemically by anaerobic bacteria - those bacteria that live and work without oxygen.

2. In the Aeration compartment the finely divided, pre-treated material is mixed with activated sludge and aerated. The aerator injects large quantities of fresh air into this compartment to provide oxygen for the aerobic digestion process.

3. The final phase of the operation takes place in the settling/clarifying compartment. In this compartment, the settling of any remaining settleable material is returned, to the aeration compartment for further treatment.

Environmental Protection - The highly treated effluent discharged from a plant is normally colorless and odorless and meets standards of larger plants. This is natural, since this watertight, self-contained plant treats wastewater in the same manner as a central treatment plant.

Effluent Disposal Simplified - Effluent disposal in any area is controlled by the health authorities. Many authorities have found the highly treated effluent eliminates the need for leaching fields or subsurface filters. In a great many areas, aerated effluent is discharged directly to a storm sewer, flowing stream, or any well-defined line of drainage.

- Large Capacity
- Handles All Modern Appliances
- Frequent Tank Pumping Eliminated
- Only A Small Space Required

The units are economical to install - with low operating cost.

Field-Proven, Accepted - The carefully engineered plant with its advanced treatment process has been providing dependable wastewater treatment for individual homes since 1955.

New effluent processing plants by the same producer are available for a complete UNI-PARK of 85 homes. These larger plants work with the same thorough process.

These plants meet or exceed all criteria for evaluating and testing household aerobic wastewater treatment systems as recommended in the National Research Council Report 586. This report gives the results of a study made for the U.S. Public Health Service. The purpose of this study was to develop criteria for evaluating and testing individual household aerobic wastewater treatment systems. The Veteran's Administration has declared this home plant acceptable for its insured home loans. In addition, these plants have been sold to he U.S. Army Corps of Engineers, U.S. Navy, U.S. Post Office and many other state and federal agencies where top quality specifications are strictly adhered to.

•Individual Home and Uni-Park Wastewater Treatment Plant **# 46**

The effluent water draining from a pollution control system will be sufficiently treated within each system (National Sanitation

Foundation Seal of Acceptance) and be used for underground drip watering of private or public vegetation.

A subsurface irrigation system of porous, flexible rubber pipe, which sweats when placed in the soil, where it acts as a wick will be used primarily to eliminate water run off from recycling systems. The capillary action of the soil draws water from the pipe, which replaces water used by trees, plants and turf. This pilary action delivers water, oxygen and nutrients uniformly through the soil directly to the roots. This pipe works with very low water pressure and has been used in agriculture e.g in citrus, vegetables, peanuts, cotton and in city and residential landscaping. The pipe systems are currently being developed for sugarcane, grapes and other row crops. Porous Rubber Pipe **# 47**

## 3. Agriculture

Uni-Sonians will make use of known natural agricultural methods known as permaculture, which is basically organic - natural gardening and farming in a more permanent system instead of year to year. In order to encourage private use of such healthful and nutritional practices for the family units in an economic manner and also for employment opportunities for UNI-CITIZEN shareholders.

In a recent seminar, three leaders of the global movement for a natural, permanent agriculture (also called permaculture) gathered at The Evergreen State College in Olympia, Washington, for the Annual International Permaculture Conference. The following is a brief description of work being done by people who are taking key roles in defining our planet's future. The

*Mother Earth News* Assistant Editor Pat Stone, conducted the interview, giving background on the three subjects:

Australian Bill Mollison created the concept of Permaculture. A gravel-voiced graybeard, Bill has a dry sense of humor, a feisty temperament, and absolute dedication to his cause. Introduced before his keynote conference speech as a "great yarn teller who's motivated thousands of people to action," Mollison has held every job from seaman to Tanzania bush researcher to senior lecturer in environmental psychology. He left that secure university position two years before retirement to blaze the permaculture trail.

To Mollison, permanent agriculture means carefully designed, sustainable systems in which the array, organization and interactions of plants and animals are the central factors. Perennial plants -- especially tree crops -- play a large role in his multi-species landscapes. A permaculture system takes much planning and a good bit of work, to set up, but it should then almost run itself.

Wes Jackson researches perennial crop mixes in Salina, Kansas. A hulking midwesterner with broad hands and a ready smile, Jackson combines a warm nature, downhome humor, and impeccable scientific scholarship (he has a PH.D. in genetics). For example, his favorite lecture title is "Herbaceous Perennial Seed-Producing Polycultures: Their Contribution to the Solution of All Marital Problems and the End of the Possibility of Nuclear Holocaust."

At his 200 acre Land Institute, Wes and his research staff are working to breed a mixture of perennial sunflower, rye, and other plants that could produce an ongoing yearly seed harvest

78

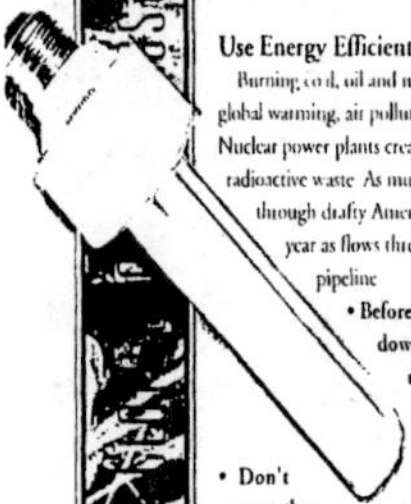

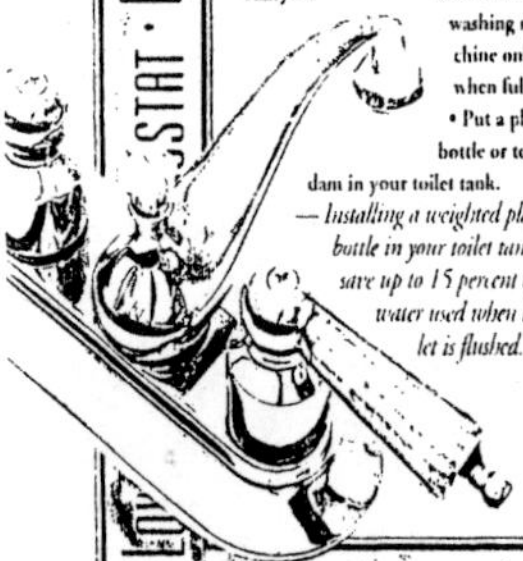

to the midwestern prairies. This high-yielding system would sponsor its own fertility, have minimal pest and weed problems and require no erosive annual tillage. The self-maintaining food system would be designed by humans but follow the principles of nature. "It's not that humans don't learn faster than nature, "Jackson says. "It's just that nature's been at it a lot longer."

Masanobu Fukuoka - it would be difficult to fully understand this fascinating man. The short, kimono-clad Oriental is essentially a Buddhist monk who has chosen the path of farming. He speaks no English, but his gentleness communicates itself at a glance. (Those twinkling eyes also reveal that a playful imp shares a place with the humble philosopher.)

Fukuoka was an agricultural scientist who, after a serious illness, had a "flash of insight" that nature was perfect, while human knowledge was meaningless. He set out to prove these ideas through farming and has been raising rice, barley and citrus on a small commercial farm since World War II. Fukuoka advocates what he call "do-nothing" farming: He has used no tillage, no fertilizer, no weeding, and no pesticides for four decades, and still achieves grain yields as high as conventional Japanese farmers. *(Mother Earth News)*.

The center of American permaculture efforts and education is The Permaculture Institute of North America. A one-year membership in PINA costs $25.00 and includes a subscription to the institute's quarterly newsletter and magazine. It is the quickest way to learn about our country's permaculture network. **# 48**

All three interview subjects have books and tapes available from PINA:

Bill Mollison's *Permaculture One* and *Permaculture Two* is available at $12.50 each.

Wes Jackson's excellent 150-page critique, *New Roots for Agriculture*, costs $6.95.

Massanobu Fukuoka's new 280-page explanation of his ideas and methods, *The Natural Way of Farming*, costs $15.95, while his earlier *One-Straw Revolution* is $3.95.

Include $1.25 for shipping and handling when ordering one or two books; $2.00 if ordering three or more.

Cassette tapes of each man's conference speech and of their joint panel is also available for $5.75 each postpaid.

For information about the book from Jackson's Land Institute, its tri-annual magazine, and ways you can support his work. **# 49**

Another fine resource guide, filled with articles and access information, is the *1986 International Permaculture Species Yearbook*, which is available for $13.75 postpaid from Yankee Permaculture. **# 50**

Other informative reading sources are:
•Jim Horne, Kerr Center for Sustainable Agriculture# **51**
•Jim Lukens, Meadowcreek Project **#52**

## a. Home Production Use
Several methods of providing fresh nutritional foods can be done on the private premises such as hydroponics, patio gardens and planting edible fruit bearing trees and shrubs.
•Videos and Instruction **# 53**

- Garden Carts # 54
- Mother Earth News # 55

### i. Patio Gardens - Formal Gardens - Cottage Gardens, Pocket Courtyards

Patio gardens provide not only beauty but also provide edibles for the table. A very little amount of space used properly can provide a large amount of fresh  produce.

Information assistance and training will be given by Uni-Citi Agra Centre in Oriental Asian gardening as  well as other  water and space saving methods.  (See Porous Rubber Pipe).

- Garden Club of America #56
- Oriental Gardening # 57

## JAPANESE/ORIENTAL GARDENS
### (from "A Japanese Touch for Your Garden"
### by Seike, Kudo, & Engel)

A pathway through pebbles in the famous garden, built by Prince Toshihiko, in 1602. (Picture from "Art of the Japanese Gardens by Talsuo Ishimoto)

## What makes a Japanese Garden?

The idea comes first, then the materials. The garden-maker may wish to suggest a woodland, with a mountain backdrop. He may want the splash of a waterfall, or the murmuring sound of a stream flowing over pebbles. Or he may dispense with water if he wishes, using stones to suggest a stream-bed.

## Shishi Odoshi

The *Shishi Odoshi* or "deer scare," was originally developed by farmers as a means of scaring off deer and wild boar that damaged their crops. Water is fed through a thin bamboo pipe into an angled length of thick bamboo which is set on an axle and whose first joint has been scraped or cut away on the inside. Water collects, and its weight forces the front tip of the bamboo to the ground; when the water runs out, the rear end of the

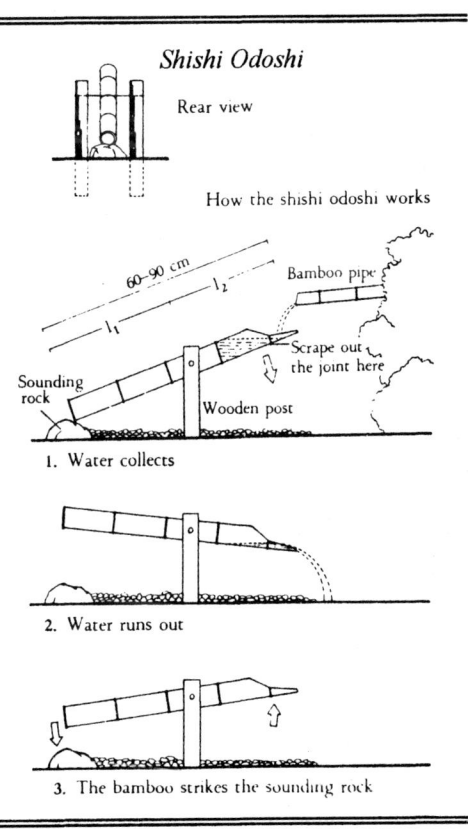

Shishi Odoshi
Rear view

How the shishi odoshi works

60–90 cm

Bamboo pipe

Scrape out the joint here

Sounding rock

Wooden post

1. Water collects

2. Water runs out

3. The bamboo strikes the sounding rock

bamboo, now heavier than the tip, drops quickly to the ground, where it strikes against a rock to produce a sharp, clacking sound. The flow of water and the regular movement of the *shishi odoshi* provide an effective counterpoint to the changelessness of the other garden elements. The sudden clack of the bamboo and its resonant dissolution suggest to some the process and effects of time.

The *shishi odoshi* is often placed on the edge of a pond, which serves to collect the water that runs off. It can also be used on slightly higher ground as a source of a stream or waterfall.

## Bridges

A bridge across a wet or dry stream bed can be an attractive addition to your garden. A bridge designed merely for decoration is not unheard of, but it is safe to assume that guests, and children especially, will have an urge to test it out. All the bridge supports should be very secure. Choose materials that are appropriate to your garden. If, for example, your garden has been designed to have an "untouched" look, a simple bridge made of rough planks might be best. If you use a lot of stone themes in your garden, make

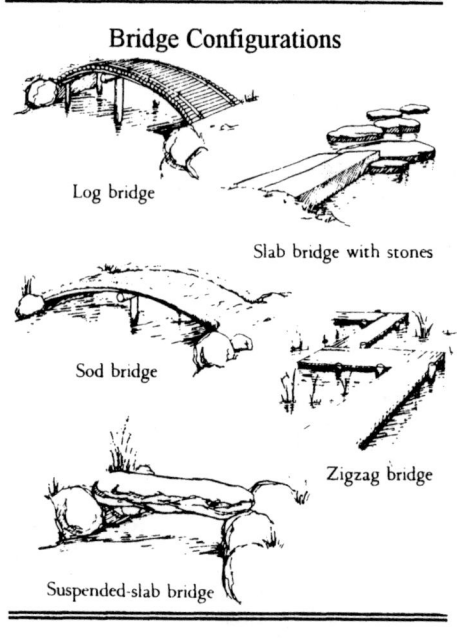

Bridge Configurations

Log bridge

Slab bridge with stones

Sod bridge

Zigzag bridge

Suspended-slab bridge

a bridge out of a single granite slab. For safety, set two rocks on each side of the apron of the bridge and a lantern nearby to illuminate it at night.

## Formal/Patio Garden

People with a considerable amount of land and the yen for a patio or formal garden may want to add significant stone features to their garden without having to expend large amounts of time, money, or labor in order to do so.

One is paid many times over by the beauty and durability stone add to any site. But there are ways to present stone constructions in formal gardens so their impact exceeds their actual dimensions.

One way is to establish formal lines in the garden by using stone features, and then to continue and extend those lines with hedges and other plantings. The rectangular shape of the garden may be established by stone walls on the short sides and evergreen hedges on the longer sides. Gravel *allees,* may be bordered on corners by clipped evergreens in painted tubs, dividing the garden into symmetrical quarters of lawn. In the center, where the *allees* meet, a pergola supporting wisteria, clematis, or roses arches over a floor made of cobbles set in mortar and bordered by pavers. The same type and size of pavers are used as a base for the benches set at the ends of the shorter *allees,* against the evergreen hedges. Large pots containing mophead hydrangeas (*Hydrangea macrophylla)* may be set next to the benches.

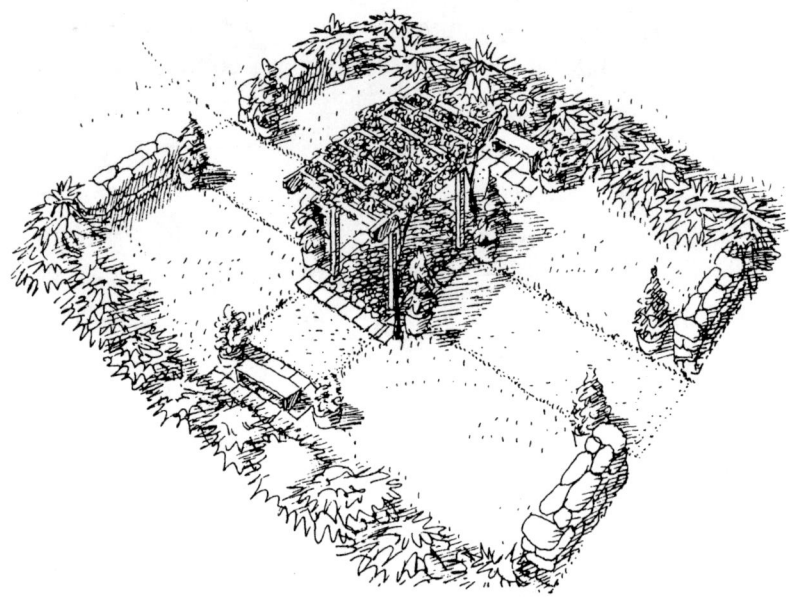

Stone walls and gravel paths establish the dominant lines in a formal garden.

## A Cottage Garden

There are few garden styles more evocative than the cottage garden. Hollyhocks and foxgloves; lilies and roses; pinks, poppies, and snapdragons; all the flowers that most stir the hearts of gardeners tumble together happily under sunny blue skies in the cottage gardens of our daydreams.

For many gardeners, these vision gardens start out at the path, leading up to the cottage's front door. Usually quite straight and narrow, the paths can be made of crazy paving, cobbles set in cement, or Belgian blocks with sand swept between them, and their margins can be lost in mounds of sweet-smelling low spreaders, such as alyssum *(Lobularia maritima)*, cherry pie *(Heliotropium peruviamum)*, and garland flower *(Daphne eneorum)*, which send up puffs of fragrance as visitors brush by them.

A path of Belgian blocks and flagstones wanders through a cottage garden.

## A Pocket Chinese Courtyard

The Chinese term for garden, *shen shui*, literally means "piling rocks and digging ponds," underscoring the importance of both elements in Chinese gardens. A pocket garden may be set in the corner of a small urban garden, with both stones and water, set off by a cobbled mosaic floor. A tree scatters light shade over the cobbles, while tufts of lilyturf *(Liriope)* spring from the base of the specimen rocks rimming a tiny pool. Ornamental pots filled with flowering peonies (traditional favorites of Chinese gardeners) can provide seasonal color and foliage.

Today many gardeners feel that the most valuable and attractive gardens they can create are wild. Serving as sanctuaries for native wildlife and plants, such gardens permit us to act as conserving links in the great chain of being and to reaffirm our ties to the land and to our fellow creatures. If you plan to create an environment in which birds, butterflies, toads, and other wildlife will flourish right outside your windows, stone features can play attractive and useful roles in the design.

Wildlife is attracted to gardens where shelter, water and food are available. The following stone features help to provide them:

•Holes under dry stone walls and naturalistic rockeries serve as shelters for squirrels, gophers, chipmunks, rabbits, lizards, and snakes. Build reinforced shelters under the walls or rockeries as you construct them, since animals can weaken their foundations if left to burrow the shelters by themselves.

•Natural-style ponds, rimmed with rocks and stones and at least 18 to 24 inches deep, will permit frogs, toads, snails, and crayfish to winter over snugly in their depths. If you pile rocks along the edge of a pond and allow others to trail into the water to a depth of several feet, they will provide shelter from predators, and also serve as basking ledges for sunny afternoons. If you place larger stones with hollows further out into the pond, they can serve as perches for birds as they drink and bathe; such isolated islands also provide cat-proof feeding areas for the birds.

**Suggested Japanese Gardens you can visit**

by Seike, Kudo and Engel, authors of "A Japanese Touch for Your Garden"

Brooklyn Botanic Garden, Brooklyn, NY
   Extensive Japanese stroll garden with pond and a replica of the Ryoan-ji garden.

Duke Gardens, Somerville, NJ (Tel: (201) 722-3700
   Acres of gardens under glass, including Japanese garden. Call first for hours and reservations.

Golden Gate Park, San Francisco, CA
   An extensive Japanese garden dating from an international exposition many decades ago.

Gulf States Paper Corporation, PO Box 3199, Tuscaloosa, AL Tel: (205) 553-6200
   A corporate headquarters, consisting of four Heian-period-style pavilions set around a Japanese garden. Call for appointment.

Hillwood Museum Gardens, 4155 Linnean Ave., NW, Washington DC
   A Japanese garden within the extensive estate of the late Marjorie Merriweather Post. May be visited, but reserve two weeks in advance. $2.00 fee with reservation. Open

Monday, Wednesday, Friday, and Saturday, 9:30-11:30 and 1:30-3:30.

The Morikami, Yamato Colony, Palm Beach County, FL
Gardens and a museum. Write the director for admission details.

Oriental Stroll Garden, Hammond Museum, North Salem, NY
Write the director for admission details.

Missouri Botanical Gardens, 2101 Tower Grove Ave., St. Louis, MO Tel (314) 865-0440
A large Japanese garden, recently completed.

Tennessee Botanical Gardens and Fine Arts Center, Cheekwood, Nashville, TN.

Ft. Worth, Texas Oriental Garden and Botanical Gardens.

## ii. Rental Gardens

Areas will be provided within the UNI- CITI similar to the garden areas in Europe on an economical rental fee. Space-saving Asian and Oriental gardening techniques will be fostered.

Community planned organic gardens, flower and herb gardens, encourage the harvesting of all available produce for purchase from the community market providing funds to keep the project maintained as well as providing natural herbicide free, healthful foods for a richer more bountiful life.

The National Association for Gardening has the perfect solution for "would be" urban and suburban vegetable growers.

•National Association for Gardening **#58**

*Mother Earth News* always carries a lot of good information like the following:

When the winter's snow has melted back to a few gritty gray piles on the street corner and the first crocuses show bright green in front of the porch, a lot of folks turn their thoughts toward putting in a garden. Unfortunately, many people who'd love to raise their own vegetables are - because of a lack of available growing space - unable to do so. However, over one million Americans have already solved the exact same problem...by forming community gardens! Such groups of vegetable raisers simply share adjacent growing plots on otherwise unused public or private land, and the crop coalitions often obtain their "growing privileges" for free!

You can found a community garden where you live, too. All it takes is a bit of organizational know-how and some enthusiasm. Of course, it'll be up to you (or to someone you know) to provide the "spark plugging" energy for such a project...but a group called the National Association for Gardening can readily supply all the "how to do it" information you'll ever need.

The dedicated organization has helped dozens of successful community growers from Boston to San Jose. And the NAG folks--who know scads of useful "inside tips" and "pitfalls to avoid"--have freely offered to share their hard-earned knowledge with MOTHER's readers.

PLAN AHEAD - You will, of course, need to work out the physical details and membership rules for your community garden before you hold a "sign up day"for growing plots. For instance, you should predetermine the size of an individual garden (NAG recommends 25' x 30' vegetable patches, because forty such plots - plus access walks - will fit in a one-acre tract, and each of the moderate-sized gardens can provide a family of four's vegetables for most of the year). You'll have to arrange for a water supply, too (check with the local fire department) and decide whether to provide tools - which may be donated by a community minded sponsor - and an on-site toolshed.

Your members should be told in advance about any fees that have been decided upon, what the consequences for neglecting their plots would be (usually the loss of growing privileges), whether organic or nonorganic growers will be separated, and where seeds and gardening information can be obtained.

You can also start the following season's public relations effort during harvest time...by holding - and publicizing - a homegrown banquet, a community food contest, a curbside "garden market", or even a charity giveaway of surplus goodies.

EDITOR'S NOTE: The National Association for Gardening has published both a 38-page paperback book, *Guide to Community Garden Organization*, and a project coordinator's job description and timetable. These materials go into detail on all the tips mentioned in this article and cover several other topics - such as "finding a sponsor," "ways around red tape," and "preventing thievery" - as well. You can get both items - for only $2.00 postpaid. In addition, you can become a member of the non-profit gardening association (and receive its quarterly news publication) for $10.00. **#59**

The Kansas City Community Gardens Project started in 1979 as a part of a hunger-outreach program through the Metropolitan Lutheran Ministries (MLM). In its early days, it worked with a staff of one and several dedicated volunteers.

•Community Gardening **# 60**
•Gardens for All **#61**


### iii. Fruits and Berries, Trees and Shrubs

Selected edible fruit producing trees and berry plants provide a lot of pleasure and beauty and enhance the environment as well as helping to control noise pollution.

Uni-Citizens will be offered information and guidance in the practical use and planting of trees and shrubs.

# Cool The Sun

Half the fun of planting a tree is imagining what it will be like in a few years. Our tree will branch out to shade us from the summer sun, help cool our home and the neighborhood, and conserve energy in the process. It will provide a home for songbirds, and will remind us of the special times we share together.

You can cool and beautify your home, too. Join me and plant a tree. For your free booklet, write: Conservation Trees, The National Arbor Day Foundation, Nebraska City, NE 68410.

**The National Arbor Day Foundation**

## b. Commercial Production

The Unisonian Citi will make use of natural agricultural production and processing methods to provide nutritional foods at economical costs while at the same time providing job opportunities for uni-citizen shareholders.

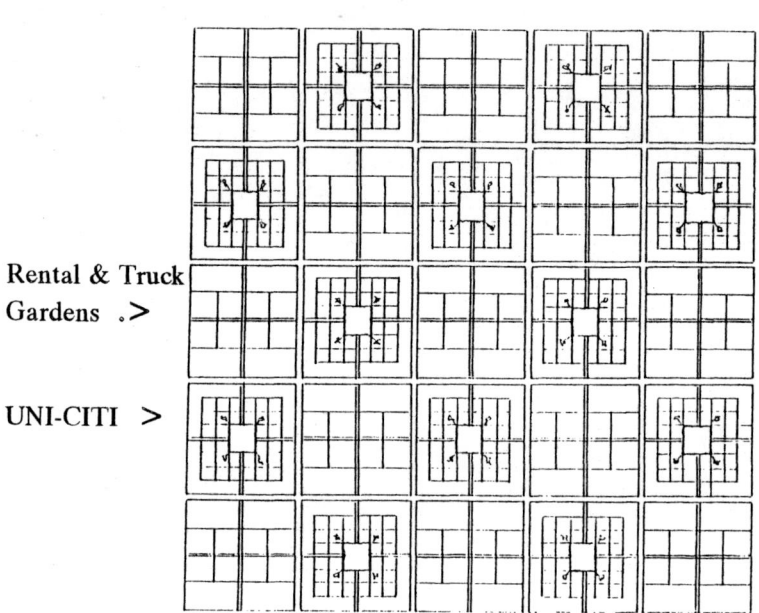

Rental & Truck
Gardens .>

UNI-CITI >

Twelve (12) UNI-CITIES could be interspersed checkerboard
patterned allowing for rental garden and truck farms.

It was Harold Wills, a former editor, wheat trader, author
and lecturer, who divided agriculture between cellular forms
and plantations. The cellular farm, he wrote, was one that is
self-contained and properly referred to as the family farm. A

plantation is a commercial enterprise where labor, hired or otherwise, does the work for an owner or owners who may not live on the land.

The uni-cellular acreage of 10 acres will be close to the Uni-Citi in the adjoining sections used for more concentrated agricultural crops. The uni-cellular acreage will be owned by the individual operator at least 60% and up to 40% by the Uni-Citi. (640 acres per section in 10-acre plots, with 20 acres for access = 62  10-acre units.

•Fallen Eagle (book by Harold Wills) **#62**

### i. Hydroponics and Greenhouses

The year around practice of hi-density planting of vegetables and irrigating with nutrient supplement for fast healthy plant growth will be encouraged. Enclosed rooftop systems are a very practical use of space as well as are other locations on private premises such as green rooms.

Vegetables and flowers will be produced for commercial resale within the citi and beyond.

•Hydroponics **# 63**
•Greenhouses **# 64**

### Water-Holding Crystals

A tool for proper water management. **# 65**

Effective water management is an absolute must for all plant life - too little water can cause severe stress and shock, too much water encourages root rot and fungus - both conditions can result in substantial plant loss and profit loss.

Water-holding crystals are a man-made, cross-linked polymer with the primary benefit of increasing the water-holding capacity. Water-holding crystals are mixed or tilled into the soil, significantly increasing the water available to your crops. They absorb up to 400 times their weight in water. Cross-linked water-holding crystals may be used for plant growth benefits. **# 66**

## ii. Trees and Shrubs

Flowering and fruit producing trees and shrubs will be grown by the UNI-CITI nursery for park areas and for resale within the community.

## iii. Multi-Use Crops

Potatoes, corn and other crops are versatile. Crops such as corn may be processed into many different use products such as ethanol additives and other processable bi-products like feeds.
•National Corn Processing Association. **# 67**
•National Corn Growers Association. **# 68**

## iv. Livestock, Poultry and Fish

People are raising rabbits and fish for a nutritious foods source while also raising rabbits for heat in green houses. Rabbits, catfish, salmon, and trout are very low in cholesterol level. Poultry will provide both nutritious meat and fresh eggs.

The office of Home Economics, State Relations of the U.S. Department of Agriculture has made extensive tests and have stated that domestic rabbit meat is the most nutritious meat known to man. Domestic rabbit meat is very low in cholesterol, more easily digested, and gives greater food value with far less waste. Rabbit on the dinner table is as economical, if not more so, as any meat you can purchase. It has very little waste, only 12 to 14 percent of the dressed carcass being waste. Rabbit meat is seasonable any month of the year and is especially recommended during the hot summer months, as it does not contain the heating properties of most all other meats.

## Why Raise Rabbits?

The prime purpose of the DOMESTIC RABBIT produced in America today is for the dinner table.

Rabbits teach our younger people animal husbandry and delight them as pets. They offer adults income and recreation and gardeners beg for the manure, which has the highest nitrogen content of all livestock manure. Besides all of the above, they furnish the American cooks at home a delectable family dish and more protein than any other meat known.

With millions of Americans turning to the soil in an effort to raise food for their tables in the face of rising prices, thousands of them are also making more than a simply vegetarian effort. They have turned to the Domestic Rabbit to fill the need for home-grown meat on the table at a fraction of the price in the supermarket. Many homeowners are turning their back lawns into vegetable gardens and also finding space for a few rabbit hutches to raise their own meat. More and more Americans find the rabbit a delight for the palate and pocketbook.

Rabbit raisers, with experience, for years have raised from 4-6 litters of 6-8 fryers each per individually caged doe (female), maintaining a stud buck for every 20 does. With a 31-day gestation period, butchering day arrives 12-14 weeks after conception. Raised under the most sanitary and controlled environment of all farm animals, these 4 to 5 lb. fryers dress out at better than 50%. Feed conversion rate of the entire herd, which includes young replacement stock, is approximately 4:1, with the feed cost to produce a pound of edible meat about $.75. Put that $.75 against a pound of anything in your market and then decide whether you have the spare time to add a few rabbits to the backyard. One doe in one hutch, can produce 70 to 95 lbs. of dressed, edible meat each year. No other animal can be kept in a space 30" x 36" and reproduce 8 to 10 times her own weight, in edible meat, in one year.

**High Protein Meat**

Protein is said to be the secret of life, since it is responsible for all of the living tissues in our bodies and the replacement of same. Protein is also recognized as playing an important part in the chemical structure of our bodies.

•The American Rabbit Breeders Association, Inc. **# 69**

All ponds practicably possible will be stocked with cat fish. All residents will be allotted evenly apportioned days to freely fish.

•Fish Farming Association **# 70**

**4. Energy - Solar, etc.**

The constancy of solar energy availability makes it imperative that this natural resource be used in whatever ways possible. Research and experimentation is recommended and encouraged. All methods of energy production and use will be studied so the determination of the most efficient and cost effective use of energy will be made.

### Passive Solar Energy

Recently, interest has been renewed in this important energy-saving concept that requires no special machinery in order to function.

Today, more homeowners are looking *at* their windows and patio doors instead of just *through* them.

Why? Because they realize that windows and patio doors, properly oriented to the sun, can supply their homes with a source of free heat.

Using windows and patio doors to collect the sun's heat is one of the basic elements in the rapidly growing concept of passive solar energy. Simply stated, a passive solar heating system uses the structure of the home, itself, to collect, store and distribute heat from the sun with very little, if any, mechanical assistance.

Passive solar isn't new. The concept has been used by man for thousands of years. However, many of the techniques were abandoned in the days of cheap energy. Only recently, with the advent of high fuel prices, has interest in this important concept been renewed.

One reason for this interest is that passive systems can save homeowners money anywhere they live. As the map shows, even in the northern parts of the country, passive solar can supply at least 30% of a home's heating needs. In milder climates, it can meet up to 80%.

Picture U

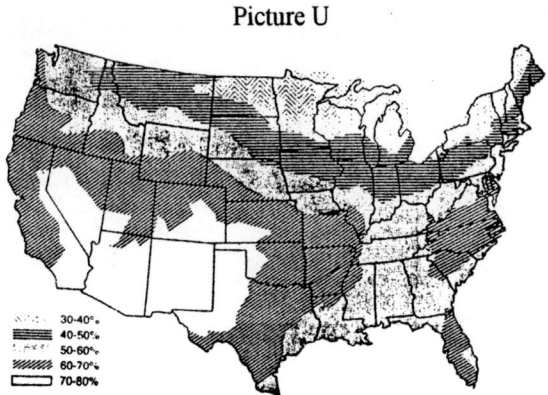

30-40%
40-50%
50-60%
60-70%
70-80%

Estimated percentage of a home's heating load that can be met through the installation of high-efficiency passive solar systems. (Source: Los Alamos Scientific Laboratory)

Actual savings, of course, will depend on the use of such non-solar energy-saving techniques as proper wall and ceiling insulation, tightfitting windows and doors, good weatherstripping and caulking, and proper use of drapes and blinds.

Savings will also depend on lifestyle, but with the rising cost of fuel, saving even a relatively small percentage on fuel bills can yield large dollar savings.

### a. Voltaics (Electric)

Park, yard and street lighting are only three practical uses for solar voltaics. All house and public roofs will provide space for electric generation panels. Any excess power may be injected into the power system for credit.

UNISONIA will be a prototype community for any solar voltaic experiments that hold potential for the UNI-CITI.
•Voltaics. # 71

## b. Passive - Active

Both passive and active solar space heat generation for public and private preheating water for domestic use, auto washing and swimming pools as well as other uses will be encouraged.

Passive and/or active solar heat will be used in ag and waste processing and other usage such as hydroponics.
•Solar Water Heaters # 72
•Solar Air Heaters # 73
•Fusion-Fission-Methanol-Ethanol-Hydrogen # 74

## 5. Transportation

The orderly movement of people, vehicles and materials is important for safety, sound control, general tranquility and well being of the uni-citizens.

All known methods of controlling noise and air pollution will be pursued, including encouragement and incentives for citizens to use non-polluting vehicles such as methanol, ethanol or electric power. When citi size permits, a transit system will be initiated.

A Monorail Tire System, with one-man operation, is electronically controlled and often used for theme parks of any size. Regular model includes three sections carrying 35 adults, but more cabs may be added. Two tracks may be used on a "T" support with the trains passing at any point; track or tracks are available in any configuration. The Motor is concealed, bearings sealed and the electronic device is said to require little maintenance. Cabs may be obtained in almost any design to fit the theme. **# 75**

For more information on AEG people mover cars or mass transit systems, contact AEG Transportation Systems, Inc., 1501 Lebanon Church Rd., Pittsburgh, Pa. 15236-1491. Telephone: 412/655-5336, FAX: 655-5860

## a. Bridges, Streets, and Motorways

All bridges, streets and motorways are designed for maximum efficiency, aesthetics and safety. The bridges will be unique and attractively out of the ordinary. San Antonio, Texas River Walk is an example. # 76

## b. Parking

The question is asked, why not do away with automobiles altogether? A nonentrophic community, needs to be accomplished through intermediate steps.

Seventy five acres of auto parks are provided around the UNI-CITI CENTRE. Five acres of parking, other than private parking spaces, are provided in each UNI-PARK. Sixty-six acres of parking is provided in the service parks for a citi- wide total of 285 landscape-enhanced acres of auto parks. Potential underground parking facilities may enhance the natural landscape with community-planted nut and fruit trees and berry bushes, for easy access from tree, to car to homemade jams and pies.

### c. Trails, Sidewalks and Lanes

Six thousand, three hundred feet of six foot wide asphalt or sand lanes in each UNI-PARK, ten miles of bicycle and walking trails beside the canal and around the circumference of UNISONIA provide easy access by biking, walking or jogging. Six thousand, nine hundred feet of sidewalks front the lots on each UNI-PARK.

Explore Minnesota 1-800-657-3700

The trails allow and encourage people to walk, bike or skate to work or do other activities within the community.

Uniquely designed rock, brick or tile walkways and patios in special interest areas are emphasized.

Attractive directional information signage will stress and insure safe use by everyone using the trails sidewalks and lanes.

Explore Minnesota 1-800-657-3700

### d. Streams and Lakes

Two miles of streams and four, five-acre lakes make it possible for Uni-citizens to paddle a canoe or a row boat within seven blocks of any residence in the citi. The lakes and streams are stocked with fish; making them more enjoyable. Aesthetic landscaping will enhance their surrounding area. Swans, geese and ducks will make the lakes their home.

Courtesty of Mrs. F. C. Russell/ Great Oak Swan Farm

•Liners for lakes and streams # 77

### B. LANDSCAPE AESTHETICS

The beauty of UNISONIA will be exceptional with the over all community natural landscape design. Uni-citizens will be provided landscape design assistance, as well as provisions for economical plantings provided by the commercial ag production service within the UNI-CITI.

Phase one landscaping on residential property will be completed prior to moving in, in accordance with the UNI-CITI addendum.

"The companies we work for are very much aware of the importance of an attractive landscape," says Peter Reelects, vice-president of the exterior division of The Spencer Co. a Houston-based, full-service horticultural firm. "They recognize over-all appearance as a very powerful marketing tool," Reelects says, and simply will not settle for less than the best.

At the Greens Point Plaza, mixed-use development in north Houston, management partly credits a spectacular landscape display for its outstanding occupancy percentage.

"We regard top-rate landscaping as a good investment in many ways," says Property Management Systems' John Sebastinas, assistant property manager at Greens Point. Sharon Hill, retail property manager at Greens Point Plaza, also sees landscaping as an attraction to retailers.

"The lush green, even in winter, and the colorful seasonal flower displays," Hill continues, "make the area attractive and inviting, softening and breaking up the expanses of concrete. Our park-like atmosphere lends an upscale feel to the complex, a feeling of security. It attracts the customers our retailers want and makes desirable impressions for our office property."

"Of course, for us the great advantage is that landscaping costs much less per square foot than lighting," Hill says. "At one of Friendswood Developments' other shopping centers, we've found that the landscaping cost-per-square-foot is about half that of all utilities combined. And the impact it has in generating traffic is tremendous."

Consider the following cost-saving tips:

1. By carefully monitoring irrigation systems, problems can often be addressed before they arise. This results in a slightly higher cost in the short run, but can save on the long-term, enormous cost of major irrigation system repairs.

2. The use of perennial flowers means that only 10 percent of the flowers may need to be replaced each year, rather than up to 100 percent.

3. Careful, skilled use of pesticides and herbicides in the early stages of pest and weed management controls problems ahead of time.

4. The contractor's choice in equipment can play a major role in cost savings. Reelects points out that best does not always mean more expensive. (Building Operating Management, January 1987, Landscape Aesthetics.)

•Natural Landscaping Design **#78**
•Landscape Management Techniques **#79**

## 1. Parks

This citi of parks provides 300 acres within the twenty-eight UNI-PARK'S eleven acres each. Each has a twenty-five acre park area with a five acre lake in each of the four quads which include the seven UNI-PARKS.

Night view of a UNI-QUAD Park

The outer service zone includes twenty-five acre wilderness parks at each corner of the citi for a total of five hundred acres which is twenty percent of the total UNI-CITI plat.

> *"At the end of each day recharge with Mother nature's setting sun - life can be wonderful if you plan it that way."*
>
> *~ Tova Borgnine*

Plant and tree starting and preparations will be through Agriculture.

Sculpture, landscape architecture, creative playground equipment will be strategically located throughout the community.

Such amenities as petting zoos will be available.
•A Junior Naturalist Program such as that of Powell Gardens at Kingsville, Mo. will be encouraged. **# 80**
•Sculpture. **# 81**
•The American Society of Landscape Architects. **# 82**
•Creative Playground Equipment **# 83**

According to Brent Saville in *Industrial Design's Annual Design Review*, the *American Institute of Graphic Arts*, and *Communications Arts* magazine -- "Nearly everyone these days appreciates the importance of play in the lives of children. But while we pay lip service to the belief, we provide equipment and environments for public playgrounds that have almost always been inimical to creative and imaginative play and virtually unusable by the nation's seven million handicapped children of school age."

Our understanding of the nature of play and its role in the physical and mental development of children and adults has increased dramatically in recent years. Few opportunities for designers of all specialties should be more fertile than developing a new outdoor, public playground specifically for the integrated play of handicapped and able-bodied children alike.

Creative Playground/Equipment

Leathers and
Associates, Inc.
Phone 607-277-1650

But even the most well-intentioned projects in this difficult area can create problems that cast doubt on their value. A case in point involves New York City, where the concept of the integrated playground is becoming a reality under the enthusiastic leadership of a special unit in the Department of City Planning under Saul Nimowitz, director. Yet, despite an abundance of energy and the best intentions, the effort has some serious flaws (primarily in conjunction with specific disabilities).

Because the design of recreation areas and facilities for the disabled is a relatively new and still limited area of the design professions, and in order to elicit the widest variety of innovative solutions, The planners secured $100,000 for the city's first Federal Community Development Block Grant to sponsor a juried design competition for a Playground for All Children.

With unusual diligence, the planning group undertook a comprehensive research study of the site and user group, which was furnished as part of the design competition.

Furthermore, the planning group obtained a contract with the Department of Housing and Urban Development (HUD) to prepare a national survey of existing recreation facilities for children with handicaps. This information was presented in an open seminar. The Eastern Paralyzed Veterans Association suggested and sponsored a concurrent competition for design students with $2,000 in prizes. They received many creative solutions to disability recreation needs.

The concept of play environments with mostly moveable materials and tools has been long and well-established in the world-wide development of (true) adventure playgrounds for able-bodied and handicapped children alike, where, rather than imaginative pieces of play equipment nicely laid out along a pathway, the playground itself, together with all of the materials in it, continually lends itself to change. For the playpark being built at National Children's Island in Washington, D.C. for example, the director, Joseph Henson, included an adventure playground with a "Constant Newness Chart" provided by the designers.

The nature of adventure playgrounds as they have evolved quite obviously offends the aesthetic sensibilities of some "grownups," and there are problems and misunderstandings for designers to solve and vast improvements to be made. But the essential features of the adventure playground would seem to be a requirement for any playpark such as this competition envisions.

If, in a popular catch-phrase, "sand and water are essentials," then surely they aren't the only moveable essentials. If "children can create their imaginary world from simple and cheap things," surely simple and cheap things must be available as part of the environment provided. If "kids have to be able to manipulate their environment," surely designers must give them a meaningfully manipulable environment. If it is not a contradiction to expect from designers that which has no fixed form--by design--then it is disappointing to find these catch-phrases recurring with so little attention paid to the design criteria they entail.

The tricentennial exhibition in Charleston, S.C. operates successfully on so many levels that it can almost be regarded as a primer for how to communicate effectively with the public. Conceived as part of an ambitious celebration effort that would

116

encompass a total of three major sites in different parts of the state, the Charleston exhibition deals with the 100-year period from the first settlement in 1670. In fact, its 180-acre site, located on a peninsula across the river from Charleston, includes the place where the first settlers landed and stayed for ten years.

Carlos Ramirez and Albert Woods, principals of the New York based firm that bears their names, used artifacts, facsimiles, film, graphics and sculptural elements to recreate 100 years of Carolina history. Working closely with Synergetics Inc., the Raleigh, N.C., firm responsible for the architecture, they created a multi-level exhibit that provides the public with a boldly sketched impression of early colonial life, while, at the same time, allowing those who have the time or interest to delve more deeply into the past and absorb the cultural heritage of colonial Southern America.

The basic assumption, however, whether or not visitors linger or just pass through, is that they will come back again and again.

Many new concepts for public interest education and enjoyment exists and may be created, such as the Educational Maze, designed by Jim Zurbrigen, Fred Silbernagle and myself. **# 84**

## 2. Lakes, Streams, Waterfalls, and Fountains

Landscaping around the lakes and along the streams, will be aesthetically pleasing and help create a tranquil atmosphere. A small lake and a waterfall will be in each UNI-PARK. Other aeration methods such as fountains in clusters of three will be used in all water  used in all water pools in order to control mosquitoes.  Martin houses will be encouraged throughout the citi in order to reduce  the insect population primarily the mosquito population.  Blue bird houses, etc. will also be encouraged to attract wildlife for song and beauty.

•Waterfalls **# 85**
•Fountains **# 86**
•Ponds, Lake and Stream Liners **# 87**

Kansas City,
A city of fountains

## 3. Lighting

Solar lighting units for parks and walkways will be possible in many interesting places because of a lack of wiring requirements. Creative lighting techniques will provide interesting and unique inspirational effects. All uni-citizens will be encouraged and assisted in using lighting to the best advantage on their private property.

•Solar Lighting. **# 88**

Dakota Dunes 712-277-7456, Edward D. Jones Jr. Associates, Planners

## 4. Fencing

All home sites will have a divider fence a minimum of four feet high, enclosing the back thirty-five feet. A chain link fence will be placed at the back of all lots with a three-foot wide hinging chain link gate entering into the park for families to contain their pets.

- Concrete Fence **# 89**
- Earthtone Chain Link Fence **# 90**
- Earthtone Panel Fence **# 91**

## 5. Motorways

The motorways will be lined by a twenty-five foot greenway on each side with interesting landscaping to buffer the homes to some degree from the traffic.

Sculpture and other art works, fountains and water-falls will be placed for maximum aesthetic effect.

## 6. Parking Areas

All parking areas will be tastefully provided with greenery and other plantings to also enhance sculptural interest and relaxation spots.

## 7. Buffer Areas

The one hundred acres of park area in the outer buffer zone will be primarily wilderness area for the enjoyment of all the uni-citizens. Nature trails, lecture facilities and camping grounds will be included.  Wildflowers and decorative plants native to the area will be spread throughout the wilderness area.  Boulders and smaller stones will be placed randomly throughout the area.

The remaining six hundred acres in the nine-hundred feet wide buffer will be used for production and service area as well as medical, vocational and religious facilities.

## C.  UNI-PARK

The UNI-PARK people-land ratio of three homesites per acre is not a heavy ratio.

The aesthetics of every UNISONIAN living adjacent to a park is one of the most enjoyable environments one can experience.

A greater ratio can be achieved per Uni-Park acre by dividing the 75 ft. square lots into 75 x 37 ½ ft. - 172 units per Uni-Park or 75 x 25 ft. - 258 units per Uni-Park.

Look for ideas in
THE SUCCESSFUL GARDEN

### UNI-QUAD Park

The look and function of Uni-quad parks are the

ultimate in demonstrating environmental considerations within the region where the Uni-Citi is located. As an example, nature trails would include different plantings, trees and earth, even stone, depending on the part of the country in which the community is established. This difference of material, of course, will create many diverse and uniquely interesting Uniquad parks.

Each Uniquad park will include a fascinating multi-use 3-acre lake which, if possible, will be connected to the waterway surrounding the city centre plaza.

The bike trails will tie into the city-wide trail system. Bikes, paddle boats and canoes may be checked out in any of the Uniquad parks free for use in recreationally transporting Unisonians wherever they would like within the community. One experiment I am aware of provided brightly colored, easily recognizable bikes.

Lighting and landscaping are other areas creative design can be used to accomplish positive attitudinal and pleasurable results.

## Service Park

The look of the service park which is an approximate 3-5 block greenway surrounding the community will include a natural park-like look.

The parking lots will be landscaped in such a way to make them pleasantly utilitarian yet environmentally supportive.

The surroundings will be a pleasant place to work and play productively and happily.

### 1. UNI-PARK Associations

Each UNI-PARK association will administer all aspects of their respective UNI-PARK. Each unit owner has one vote in the affairs of their own UNI-PARK and the UNI-CITI. Therefore, everyone has equal input.

Please refer to Dedication and Specification Covenants following.

### DEDICATION AND SPECIFICATION COVENANT

### THE UNISONIAN UNI-PARK/UNI-CITI PLAN ENVIRONMENTAL AND LAND USE PROTECTIVE COVENANTS

The Grantors realizing that protective covenants are essential to the sound development of suburban areas in that they contribute to the establishment of the character of a neighborhood and to the maintenance of value levels through the regulation of type, size and placement of buildings, lot sizes, reservation of easements and prohibition of nuisances and other land used that might affect the desirability of a residential area hereby enact the following protective covenants:

1.    Said lot shall be restricted to single-family dwellings. No lot shall be subdivided unless approved by the UNI-CITI structures design unit building committee in situations such as row houses across from each UNI-PARK Activity Center and shops.

2.    The exterior of each dwelling commenced shall be completed, together with all grading, within six months

from the date of first excavation.

3. Said lot shall be considered too small, therefore, the owners shall not graze livestock. A petting zoo lot for livestock shall be permitted by the UNI-CITI and/or any UNI/PARK. No dog kennels shall be permitted. All animals must be controlled to owners property or be controlled by the UNI-PARK Board.

4. No trash burning or dumping. All trash must be collected by UNI-CITI water resource management unit with the exception of leaves and grass which will be composted. No litter will be allowed to scatter. Containers with lids will be kept in a sanitary manner. Aluminum, other metals, glass, plastic items, miscellaneous waste will be separated as each householder places waste in provided containers in UNI-PARKS. All lawns must be kept in A-1 condition which includes natural landscaping.

5. No building shall be located on any lot nearer than 20 feet to the front line, and 12 feet to the one side with shared wall of all lots except the 25 ft. x 75 ft. lots which will be to the lot line on one side and no closer than 4 ft. on the other on the first floor; the second floor may be line to line.

6. All effluent systems shall be not less than 1,000 gallon capacity and have accessory attachment to chlorinate water run off to adequately service said dwelling and must meet the requirements of recommendations of the State Health Departments.

See ENVIRONMENTAL, LAND USE - EFFLUENT -

Jet System. All dwellings will use flush toilets of two quarts or less water.

7. All of the foregoing restrictions shall run with the land and shall be binding upon all owners for a term of ten years, and successive periods of ten years, unless amended or added to at the end of any ten-year period, in accordance with provisions hereof.

8. Any dwelling constructed on this lot shall be constructed in a workman-like manner of materials to be approved by the UNI-CITI Structures and Facilities Design Unit before constructions. A one, two, three or four bedroom home shall contain no less than 1,500 square feet of living space. Living space shall not include garages, carports, storage areas or basements. The square footage of the second story of a two-story house shall count for one half in determining minimum square footage restriction.

9. No temporary basement houses, no tents or shacks are to be erected. No old house to be moved onto said lot. No temporary structures except construction sheds, which are to be moved before occupancy of dwelling. No mobile homes are permitted. Construction of all outbuildings must be approved by the Structures and Facilities Design Unit.

10. No slaughter houses, auto salvage yard, junk yard or other industrial enterprise from which offensive odors may arise shall be permitted or constructed on any of said lots. No noxious or offensive activity shall be done thereon which may or may not become a nuisance to the

neighborhoods. The same guidelines extend into the UNI-PARK COMMON LAND.

11. The owner of said lot bought and not built on at once must be responsible for maintaining said lot or pay UNI-CITI Environmental Land Use Unit for same. Three years from date of purchase, buyer must complete dwelling or said property will revert back to the UNI-CITI.

12. No fence, wall or hedge in front of property shall be more than four feet in height, unless authorized in writing by the UNI-CITI Structures and Facilities Design Unit, or unless such wall is built as part of the house within the areas specified for house location.

13. Solar collectors for electro-voltaic and or water heating is required on each home and may be provided by the UNI-CITI corporation.

14. Restrictions shall be enforced by UNI-CITI developers, their heirs, or assigns, or any owner of lots in said UNI-PARK sub-division, as divided by injunctions, mandamus or other proceedings at law or in equity against the present or future party or parties infringing, violating, attempting to infringe or violate or omitting to abide by said restrictions, and in addition thereto, and present or future owner or owners, occupant or occupants of said land or any part thereof may recover damages for the breach, infringement or violation of any such restrictions.

These restrictions may be amended, repealed or added to by owners of a majority of the lots in said UNI-CITI or UNI-PARK. If not within a UNI-CITI, it shall not be necessary that these covenants be referred to in any subsequent deeds of conveyance.

Following is another choice of a DEDICATION AND SPECIFICATION COVENANT tailored for UNI-CITI developments:

## UNISONIAN Environmental Land Use
## DEDICATION AND RESTRICTIONS

The State of_____ )

County of_____ )

_____ Unisonian Parks, Inc., the Owner of all that land described in EXHIBIT "A" attached hereto, hereby adopts the map attached hereto as its plan for subdividing the same, to be known as: Lots 1 through 86, Block _____.

## I. DEFINITIONS

The word "Plot" as used herein means a single piece or parcel of land out of one or more lots or parts of one or more lots approved by the Dedicator as a building site. No lot or lots shall be subdivided without the express written permission of the Dedicator.

The word "Association" as used herein shall be understood to mean and refer to the _____ UNI-PARK OWNERS ASSOCIATION.

The word "Dedicator" as used herein shall be understood to mean _____ Uni-Citi Development, Inc.

## II. RIGHT TO ENFORCE

Dedicator shall have the right to enforce the covenants and restrictions herein set forth, for its benefit and the benefit of the owners of all the property contained in this Dedication, their respective legal representatives, heirs, successors and assigns.

The restrictions herein set forth shall run with the land and be binding upon the Dedicator, its successors and assigns, and all parties claiming by, through or under it shall be taken to hold, agree and covenant with the Dedicator and its successors in title, and with each of them, to conform to and observe all restrictions and covenants herein as to the use of said lots and the construction of improvements thereon but no restrictions or covenants herein set forth shall be personally binding on any corporation, person or persons except in respect to breaches committed during its, his or their seizing of or title to said land Dedicator, or owners of any of the above land shall have the right to sue for and obtain an injunction prohibitive, or mandatory, to prevent the breach of or to enforce the observance of the restrictions and covenants above set forth, in addition to the ordinary legal action for damages, and failure of the Dedicator or the owners of any other lot or lots shown on said map to enforce any of the restrictions or covenants herein set forth at the time of violation shall in no event be deemed a waiver of the right to do so at any time thereafter. Dedicator, or its assigns, shall not be liable for any decision or action or failure to act under the provisions or covenants set out herein.

## III. DURATION

All of the restrictions and covenants herein set forth, save as the same may be changed pursuant to the provisions of this Dedication, shall continue and be binding upon the Dedicator, its successors and assigns, and all parties claiming by, through or under it for a period of twenty-five (25) years from the date this instrument is filed for record in the Office of the County Clerk of _____County, _____, and shall automatically be extended thereafter for successive periods of fifteen (15) years provided, however, that a majority of the owners of the fee title to the lots contained in this Dedication may agree to change or amend said covenants and restrictions, in whole or in part, by executing and acknowledging an appropriate agreement in writing for such purpose and filing the same in the manner then required for recording land instruments at least one (1) year before the expiration of the first twenty-five (25) year term or the expiration of any subsequent fifteen (15) year period thereafter.

## IV. HOMEOWNERS ASSOCIATION

Upon the sale by Dedicator of each lot, the owner thereof

shall be conclusively presumed to have affirmatively agreed to participate in _____ Uni-Park OWNERS ASSOCIATION, including the payment of all annual and special assessments, and purchaser agrees to join said Association and comply with all its covenants and conditions, and such participation in the Association shall be a covenant running with the land and binding upon the heirs, successors and assigns of the purchaser. Such Owners Association is a non-profit _____ corporation, and the Articles of Incorporation of such corporation provides as follows:

"Article VIII. The membership of this Corporation shall consist of every person or legal entity who is, or may hereafter become, the record owner of a fee interest to a residential lot in said _____ UNI-PARK, provided however, that any such person or entity who holds such interest merely as security for an obligation shall not be a member. Any member who sells, or otherwise disposes of (by operation of law or otherwise) such interest required for membership shall thereupon cease to be a member of the Corporation and any office which such member shall have held or any office an agent of such member shall have held, shall be vacated by such cessation of membership."

"In the event a lot in such subdivision shall be owned by more than one person, the membership rights held by the entire ownership of such lot shall constitute only one membership hereunder and each such fractional owner shall own and be entitled to vote only the fractional membership interest owned by such member."

## V. USE OF LAND

Only one single-family residence and incidental outbuilding shall be constructed or permitted to remain on any lot or plot.

No lot or plot and no residence or outbuilding located thereon shall ever be used for other than a single-family residence or purposes incidental thereto.

No garage or outbuilding on any lot or plot shall be used as a residence or living quarters, temporarily or otherwise, except by an employee engaged on the premises, or at the discretion of the Dedicator. No dwelling shall be occupied in any manner at any time prior to completion. The work of constructing the dwelling shall be prosecuted diligently from the commencement thereof until completion.

The foregoing restrictions shall not be construed to prevent the construction on any portion of said lots of a summer house, pagoda, or pavilion, or like structure, or a stairway of a private bath house, provided that such structure, shall correspond in style and architecture to the main dwelling, and said structure shall not exceed twenty feet above the ground which the same may be constructed, and such structure shall be designed and used exclusively for the convenience of the occupants of the residence theretofore constructed on the lot upon which the same is located.

## VI. FRONTAGE

Every dwelling erected on any plot shall present a good frontage on the street and every dwelling erected on corner plots shall present good frontage on both streets.

No garage, or other structure designed or intended to be used for the storage or housing of automobiles or other vehicles, shall be constructed in such way as that the doors, or openings thereof, will face toward the street; except that the Dedicator may allow exceptions to this provision if, in its exclusive discretion, it deems fit.

## VII.  BUILDING LINES

No dwelling, outbuilding, or other structure, or any part thereof, shall be erected or maintained on any plot nearer to the right of way of the adjoining street or streets than twenty five feet, but the Dedicator may in its sole discretion, change the building lines if it sees fit.

## VIII.  CONSTRUCTION

The exterior of every dwelling, including attached garages but exclusive of roofs, windows and doors, shall be approved by the Dedicator. Roofs shall be of any roofing material approved by the Dedicator.

The material used in the greenhouses shall be of the same material as required in the residences, unless substitute material is approved by the Dedicator.

The improvements constructed on every plot shall include the paving of all driveways and parking areas on the plot, in their entirety, with either concrete or asphalt concrete surfaces.

## IX. APPROVAL OF PLANS

No buildings, fences, retaining walls, walls, terraces or other structure shall be commenced, erected, or maintained, nor shall any addition, or change or alteration therein be made, unless plans and specifications, plot plans and grading plans or other information concerning the same which is satisfactory to the Dedicator, shall have been submitted to and approved by the Dedicator. A copy of all such plans, specifications and other written information shall be left with the Dedicator after approval thereof by it. The approval of the Dedicator shall be required as to the material, type of construction, the location and height of any such building, fence, wall, terrace, or other structures or additions, as well as changes and alterations thereto.

## X. RIGHT TO ASSIGN

Dedicator shall have the right to assign to the Association its right to enforce the covenants and restrictions herein set forth and its right to the approval of Plans as specified in Paragraph IX above and shall have the right to grant to the Association the exercise of any of its discretionary powers.

The right to enforce said covenants and restrictions, to approve plans and to exercise its discretionary powers shall remain in the Dedicator and shall not pass to the Association until (1) assignment of such rights to the Association by written instrument recorded in the Deed Records of _____ County, _____, or (2) until the Dedicator shall be voluntarily dissolved by its shareholders or until its charter is revoked by judicial action, or (3) if Dedicator shall have disposed of substantially all of its interest in the residential lots in _____ Uni-Park and shall refuse or fail to exercise such rights for the benefit of the owners of the property contained in this Dedication.

## XI. EASEMENTS RESERVED

No building or other permanent structure shall be erected or maintained on any part of any area designated  area upon which the Dedicator may reserve an easement for utilities in any deed or deeds executed by it; but the owners of plots may erect and maintain a fence, wall or hedge along the property line within such easements, but subject at all times to the prior right to use such area for the purposes for which such easements are reserved.

## XII. CREATION OF THE LIEN AND PERSONAL OBLIGATION OF ASSESSMENTS

Each purchaser and owner of any lot by virtue of the conveyance to him by Dedicator and on behalf of his successors in title whether or not it shall be expressly set out in any deed or other conveyance, shall be deemed to have covenanted and agreed to pay to the Association all annual assessments and special assessments as hereinafter provided.  Such annual and special assessments, together with interest thereon and cost of collection of same, shall be a charge upon the lots and shall constitute a lien upon the particular lot against which each such assessment is made, and shall be a personal obligation of the person or persons who was or were the owner of such property at the time the assessment fell due.

## XIII.  PURPOSES OF ASSESSMENTS

The assessments herein provided shall be used exclusively for the following purposes, to wit:

a. To maintain, preserve and promote the beautification and utility of the waterways abutting the property covered by this Dedication; and/or

b. The regulation of plant growth, and debris accumulation; and/or

c. The control of the breeding and proliferation of mosquitos and other pests; and/or

d. The enforcement of the restrictions and covenants impressed by this Dedication; and/or

e. The maintenance of all community facilities, whether public or not, or any facilities owned by the Association for the benefit of the various lot owners, such as, but not limited to, picnic areas, open greens and pedestrian pathways.  Nothing contained herein shall limit the power of the Association to acquire other properties for development for these purposes.

## XIV. BASIS AND AMOUNT OF ANNUAL ASSESSMENT

The annual assessments shall accrue according to the calendar year, and shall be due on the first day of January following the year of accrual and shall be payable no later than the 15th day of February of that same year.  The amount of the initial annual assessments shall be as follows:

$40.00 per year - vacant lots

$60.00 per year - lots with construction

No assessments shall accrue on any lots as long as such lots are owned by the Dedicator and assessments shall accrue only on residential lots. Dedicator, in its discretion, may waive all assessments as to all lots in the entire Addition as long as the Dedicator owns the fee simple title to a majority of the lots in said Addition.

## XV. SPECIAL ASSESSMENTS

In addition to the annual assessments specified in Paragraph XLV hereof, the Association may levy at any time a special assessment for the purpose of defraying, in whole or in part, the cost of any construction, repair or replacement of any structure or facility connected with, or capital improvement relating to, the Lake System PROVIDED that any such special assessment shall have the assent of at least two-thirds of the membership, voting in person or by proxy, at a meeting duly called for that purpose. Dedicator, by virtue of its ownership of any lot or lots, shall not have a vote as to any special assessment. Any special assessment by the Association shall specify the due date there of and a date not less that forty-five (45) days thereafter when such assessment shall be delinquent, but in no case not more than double the annual assessment.

## XVI. INCREASE IN AMOUNT OR CHANGE IN BASIS OF ANNUAL ASSESSMENT

The Association may increase the amount or change the basis or the annual assessment specified in Paragraph XV hereof for any future period, provided that any such increase or change shall have the assent of at least two-thirds of all lot owners, excluding those lots owned in fee simple title by the Dedicator, voting in person or by proxy, at a meeting duly called for that purpose.

## XVII. ENFORCEMENT AND COLLECTION

Any assessment, annual or special, which is not paid on or before the delinquency date shall bear interest at the rate of ten percent (10%) per annum, and the Association may bring an action at law against the owner or person obligated to pay the same or to foreclose the lien against that property, and there shall, in any event, be added to the amount of such assessment a reasonable attorney's fee to be fixed by the Court, together with all costs of the enforcement action.

Alternatively, if the association member and the association directors deem appropriate, members in arrears may through work within the association UNI-PARK, arrange payment for the unpaid assessment.

# LOESCH

# PART III
## COMMUNICATIONS AND COMPUTERIZATION

One of the most important considerations in any concept, organization or group is in fostering open communication. The UNISONIAN Master Plan is designed to make maximum use of the numerous media available in order to offer fulfilling growth opportunities whenever possible.

> *"Luck is a matter of preparation meeting opportunity."*
>
> ~ Oprah Winfrey

**Personal Computers in UNISONIA:**

Allen Burlson states, the advent of the 80's, the Personal Computer (PC) is well-documented; its uses in the home, industry and the office of today need not be justified. While many of the conceptual uses of the PC in the home may remain unfulfilled, its true uses continue to expand exponentially. Dedicated micro-processor(s) are preferred over the PC as the BRAIN of the home. Controlling the energy use, managing the security system, and watering the lawn are but a small segment of the chores for which these devices can, and should, be utilized by the developers. The flexibility of the PC, or better still, the PC in the hands of a trained INDIVIDUAL, is most profound. Some of the beneficial functions of the PC may be as follows:

**Shopping**

Using the PC to prepare a grocery list from the selected menus of the week is now available. The list will be a total composite of the items and servings required for each dish of the menu. The compiled list will note the calories and cholesterol intake of the menu and allow the maker to adjust any dishes that are high contributors to the undesired factors. The finished list will then be sorted based on the isle arrangement of the store and printed for the shopper. For those who desire, the list may be transmitted to the store, the order selected auto-window or delivered for those confined to the home. Only the unimaginative could not envision this same concept being used for the pharmacy and other areas like merchandising.

**Mail**

Electronic-mail and message handling are highly developed technologies. In the home, scanners and facsimile devices would provide hard-copy capability for those who desired such security. 3M, a well-known manufacturer of facsimile units, has demonstrated the economies of scale required for this development by contracting the French Public Utility Commission (PUC) for home units. This was some ten years ago. Communication utilities, AT&T and MCI, are now providing software interfaces to the major MAIL product of today, E-Mail. The home telephone and the PC are all that is required to take advantage of this concept. EFT, Electronic Funds Transfer, on their PC allow all of the home owners' bills to be paid without the writing of any checks. Credit card purchases may be made using home shopping programs on the complexes' closed circuit TV channel. The savings of time, paper and postage would be phenomenal.

### Home Automation and Energy Control

The system monitors and controls many different functions in your home such as heating, cooling, lighting, appliances as well as security, safety, engineering management, and convenience. This system will save on the high cost of energy.

The system is a high tech microcomputer-controlled system that was designed to be just one of the family - that performs all those duties that take so much time out of your day.

The technology will provide homeowners with a house that's less costly and more convenient to operate. It will also provide more personal security and safety.

Smoke and fire detection can be possible in every room. Home occupants can be shown the fire's location; even the doors and windows can be monitored and locked from remote locations.

Comfort: The system can monitor and control temperature, humidity and indoor air quality to insure an energy-efficient environment. The house is heated and cooled by a zoned room-by-room energy efficient heat pump.

Security: Sensors can alert police, fire, medical services and homeowners (at work or home) of any danger or critical need. The system lets one know if a door or window has been left open or unlocked.

Economy: Maximum management of lighting, appliances, heating and cooling is achieved through direct, remote or automated control. Energy consumption of heating, cooling, water heating and major appliances or the entire house is constantly monitored and is accessible on video display.

Convenience: Plug an appliance into an outlet in any room and its operation can be directly, remotely or automatically controlled. All lights and appliances can be controlled by the touch-screen TVs or from the comfort of the living room by using a hand-held remote controller on the large screen TV. All exterior doors can be locked with electric door locks by means of the touch screen or hand held-controller.

Additional Features: Video/audio door bell, remote exterior TV camera, automatic programmable mood lighting are included. The entire house system may be operated by telephone, either remote or cellular car phone. Energy efficient facade and garden lighting enhance the home's exterior.
•Smart Home System # **92**


**Telecomputer Commuters and Home Computerized Office**
Influenced by Alvin Toffler and Marshall McLuhan, Josh L. Wilson, Jr. of Eaglecrest, California, believes "The information age will be dominated by telecommuters who need not leave their homes to work. The homes will be wired for computers, data transmission to distant offices and communications within the village."

The value of the PC in the home will be limited only by the ability of the developer/contractor and the user to conceive and utilize the available technology. These approaches will be but dividends to the work enhancement aides currently available; i.e. word processing, spreadsheet and database management systems. To dream of the uses is to implement, to need is but to fulfill a dream. This technology grows so rapidly, that the unresolved of today is the old hat of tomorrow.

**Computerized Home Office**

The One-Person Office is tailored to meet the needs of 90 percent of home-office and small-business professionals," according to Fred Blechman in his review of the Betterworking Home Office. Blechman continues, "The migration from the office to the office-at-home is changing the landscape of working America. Over 30 million professionals will be self-employed by 1992."

"Almost overnight, a new market has sprung up. Writers, consultants, contractors, designers, and others who strike out on their own ..." this system, "provides freelance professionals with a fully integrated framework that tracks project and client expenses, invoices, sales contacts, customer mailing lists, expenses and sales tax reports, and more. It is not for a retail establishment, and does not produce payroll or profit/loss statements, but does provide the necessary information for income tax preparation."

Blechman continues, "It provides users with an integrated method of tracking expenses and billing their clients accordingly, and recording invoice payments, balances and sales tax."

"While many one-person businesses operate from small rented offices, most have home offices." Blechman said.
•Telecommuter Computer System **# 93**
•Computerized Home Office **# 94**
•One-Person Office **# 95**

The developers must avail themselves of a firm current knowledge in the technology of the Personal Computer as this project comes to fruition to ensure the PC has its proper place in this project.

## A. EDUCATIONAL

Communication is always an integral part of effective educational programming. UNISONIA will network all possible media in presenting educational opportunities to all uni-citizens.

Heavy focus in all the arts will help promote and influence our creative right side of the brain in balance with structured left brain activity.

### 1. Television - Video - Radio

Television opens the world of knowledge to students. Being a picture media, it is an excellent learning tool together with the printed word.

Video-television in combination is a very effective learning tool which creates enthusiasm in the participants, opening doors to the future for the learned students.

Video opens the curtain to drama and other fine arts opportunities.

Radio is a proven media for certain aspects of education. Creativity in development of radio usage for educational purposes will be encouraged.

From "how to" shows on gardening, fishing and cooking, to city council meetings and local history programs -- older people are becoming involved in the production and presentation of local community cable TV. A video provides practical information on how to write, produce and direct local cable TV programs, influence the kind and quality of local TV, and make a valuable contribution to the community.

•For 20-minute video **# 96**

•see also **# 97**

## 2. Educational Computerization

All homes will have a computer centre which will be networked with the main computer of UNISONIA and tied into computer connection world wide.

•Worldwide Computer Connection **# 98**

## 3. Library

All ways possible will be pursued to provide a sizeable library to all uni-citizens including bookmobile and other special programs and services.

Access to computerized books for reading from personal TV screens will encourage everyone to read  much more.

David P. Brehmer says "The written word is very powerful; education must begin at home but to aid this quest libraries will be able to, upon request, acquire any literature UNISONIAN children or adults are interested in to stimulate, enhance and/or advance in their particular interests. By making all literature available through a mobile exchange program and making parents aware of such, our children's individual growth potential can be realized." Successful programs of cooperation between the public library and senior centers, nursing homes, residences for the elderly, and other senior facilities have been achieved.

•Information **# 99**

## 4. Paper Printed Materials

A UNISONIAN paper will be available to all homes, via computer viewing on TV screen or printout, with primarily local interest filling many needs of a progressive citi, but not intended to take the place of metropolitan dailies. Larger papers are brought into the home by modem as well.

## B. SECURITY AND PUBLIC INFORMATION

Security and public information are a paramount need in any community. Communicating helpful information to the uni-citizen, an attitude of care and concern for true peace and justice for all, will be the attitude of his department.

## 1. Television, Scanning, Video, and Radio

Each UNI-PARK may be equipped to offer parents and guardians TV scanning of the different areas within the parks so guidance can be given to children on over-crowded areas or other potential problems.

Video may be used well for training in the security and public information service to offer driver training and education on UNI-CITI traffic and other safety training such as bicycle, cycle, canoe, etc.

Radio is an important contact for the security and public information service.

## 2. Computerization

Fire, weather, security warnings and other such uses can be transferred through the computer modem in each home.

## 3. Library

The library provides a constant source and location of public information availability.

## 4. Paper-Printed Material

Another method of bringing security and public information to the Uni-citizen.

## 5. Postal

Each UNI-CITI home will have a locked postal box located in a cluster in the same general areas of the recycling collection points. The UNI-PARK Association may choose to arrange delivery.

•Cluster Postal Boxes **# 100**

## 6. Public Relations

A positive public relations influence through several of the above media within the security and public information service can foster a positive attitude within the UNISONIAN community.

## C. ENTERTAINMENT

The activities of the UNI-PARKS, UNI-CITI CENTRE and Service Centre will be coordinated as much as deemed advisable and to the extent desired by the participating   organizations.

### 1. Television - Video - Radio

Activities of the UNI-PARKS and or UNI-CITI may make use of the closed circuit, cable TV within the  UNI-CITI with entertainment such as ballet, rock  concerts, and magic acts.
•Comprehensive Cable TV Software Information **# 101**

Video is one of the most modern opportunities for creative and educational entertainment.  Every coordinated effort will be made to magnify its positive productive use.

As an example, many  recreation uses such as instruction in golf,  archery, skating, and cross country ski basics are shown.

Use of the radio will be encouraged for use by the schools as an entertaining, educational aid and in  other beneficial ways such as background music which would be useful in many occasions, helping to create an aura of positivity, enthusiasm, peaceful, open-hearted friendly and communicative environment.

### 2. Computerization

Computers are a popular method of entertainment which can work positively in education.

### 3. Library

A source to check out books, records, and paintings, which is interesting entertainment to many people.

### 4. Paper - Printed Materials

A primary feature of UNISONIA is the offer of multiple opportunities for creative learning and broad educational experiences including entertainment.

# PART IV
## ADMINISTRATIVE SERVICES

Every successful enterprise must possess capable and conscientious, management personnel. UNISONIA will draw far sighted, creative, positive minded, people

*"The way to have a better tomorrow is to start working on it today."*
*~Anonymous*

oriented management because of its very nature and because of the precepts on which it is based.

## A. ADMINISTRATION

The basic administration of the UNISONIAN UNI-CITI will be a mutual cooperative, nonprofit, shareholder corporation which owns the public aspects of the community. All home lots are privately owned. Each lot owner holds one share of stock in the UNI-CITI corporation. A Board of Directors, elected one from each UNI-QUAD and one from the commercial and service zones will administer the citi through a trained citi manager.

The management of a city is characterized by the substance, participants, and style (form) of the management process. The participants in the governing process can vary from a part-time city council to a team of full-time professional department managers that make up the city's Board of Directors (Council). The merits of each form of city government are commonly known and so are the short comings.

An annual meeting will be held with each of the UNI-PARK Representatives and Service Park Representatives making recommendations for the coming year and beyond. Town meetings will be held on a regular basis so participation will be at highest possible levels.

*"The impersonal hand of government can never replace the helping hand of a neighbor"*

**~ Hubert H. Humphrey**

Participants - The intended population of UNI-CITI will insure an ever present pool of ideal candidates for the limited number of positions of the recommended part time council. The individuals who elect to give of their time to insure the proper functioning of the city agencies will bring a full portion of varied management and operative skills to the council.

Style - The recommended government style for UNI-CITI is that of the part-time council. The council will employ the necessary professionals to administer the various agencies of the city. This will include fire and police protection, water and sewer, streets and parks, municipal courts, and administration. This style will provide the city with the dual benefit of the experience of the council members and knowledge of the professional staff.

The Center for Holistic Resource Management provides the tools to give direction to local governmental entities.

Holistic Resource Management is a process of goal-setting, decision-making, and monitoring, that is helping people throughout the world restore the vitality of their communities and the natural resources on which they depend.

Individuals, families, communities, tribal councils, and government agencies are turning to holistic management as a practical way to manage land, human and financial resources. Their efforts to take a holistic approach to managing resources have brought many benefits, including:
- Stronger and healthier families and communities;
- The end to long-standing conflicts over resource use;
- Increased biodiversity and productivity on the land;
- Reduced chemical inputs and expenditures;

- Pride in playing a part in restoring earth's natural processes;
- Knowledge that their land can sustain future generations.

Holistic Resource Management has proven successful because it places the responsibility for making decisions about resource use on all the people who will be affected by the decisions. These people are all part of the "whole" to be managed. That whole includes also the land, wildlife, water, soil, and vegetation, and the financial resources available to the people. Decisions, then, are based on how this whole will be affected by any single change to one of its parts.

In this, holistic management departs radically from current decision-making in resource management, which is based on mechanical models - fixing parts in isolation from the whole. Holistic management teaches people to pinpoint and address the causes of land, wildlife, and financial deterioration rather than applying "quick fix" Band-Aids to the symptoms.

## Building Community

Ensuring that everyone affected is involved means bringing people together and giving them a voice in the long-term purpose for which the land and the money will be managed. This process opens up deep new reservoirs of human creativity and productivity. and while at times it can seem unrealistic and overwhelming to include

*Goals*
*"If one advances confidently in the direction of his dreams, and endeavors to live the life which he has imagined, he will meet with a success unexpected in common hours."*

**~ Henry David Thoreau**

everyone in the goal-setting process, it is essential to the success of a holistic approach.

Once the "whole" - people, land, money - is determined and brought together, the first step in holistic management is setting a goal. This goal reflects the whole by including:
1. the future quality of life desired by the people;
2. the forms of production they must achieve from the land to support their quality of life;
3. a vision of what the land must look like to sustain their production and that of future generations.

This initial goal-setting process is one of the key elements for success. First, it reveals the many common desires and needs that we have as human beings - things like happy families, quality education, and a healthy environment in which to live. Thus, it builds a common base from which a community can work. Second, it keeps people from starting out by discussing "how" they are going to achieve some goal or "fix" some problem - an approach that leads immediately to conflict over tools or strategies.

**Plotting the Course**
Once the goal is clear, the holistic management model provides a framework within which to test each action being considered to see how it will affect the whole and whether it will move the community toward its goal. A series of questions is explored, including: Will this action undermine the ecosystem? Will it create social or cultural conflicts for anyone involved? Is it addressing the key obstacle, at the time, to moving the community toward its goal? Will it provide the best return on the money invested?

These questions are designed to make each decision ecologically, economically, and sociologically sound. The answers to these questions reveal whether an action is or is not sound.

Holistic Resource Management is constantly under research and development by the Center for Holistic Resource Management, a not-for-profit organization dedicated to restoring the vitality of communities and natural resources. The Center offers training directly to communities and to other agencies and organizations that work with land-based peoples. The backbone of its support is provided by 11 branches in the United States, Canada, Mexico, and Africa and by a loose network of organizations that share its goal of restoring the vitality of natural resources and human communities.

The Center was established in 1984, based on the work of Allan Savory, a wildlife biologist from Zimbabwe with 30 years of experience in resource management. The bulk of Savory's work has revolved around grassland and desert environments - stemming from a lengthy personal search for decertification. For years, he worked with land owners and managers the world over to encourage them to increase Biodiversity as the key to halting the deterioration of soil, plant, animal and water resources. This work increasingly led Savory to a "holistic" approach - to the process that today incorporates the people, the land, and the financial resources available. As such, Holistic Resources Management represents an ethical decision-making process that can be universally practiced by those who recognize that the basis of our survival is health of our ecosystem and the strength of our human communities.

•Holistic Resource Management # 102

The UNI-CITI planners are encouraged to insure that the

government is participative.  Each adult citizen of the city will desire to vote in all municipal elections, attend council meetings and stand for council membership as may be appropriate.  By doing so, the Management of UNI-CITI will be a major contributor to the favorable life style of the city.

•National Planners Association **# 103**

The administration is constantly thinking and acting on behalf of all age groups in the UNI-CITI. An example of this type of activity took place in the City of Tucson, the Pima Council on Aging, and the Arizona Long Term Care Gerontology Center (University of Arizona) jointly participated in a planning study with city government department heads to improve city services to older people. This unique planning approach resulted in a city blueprint for training of city employees and identification of new services critical to maintain a high quality of life for Tucson's elders.

*"A hunch is creativity trying to tell you something."*
~ **Frank Capra**

•Information **# 104**

## 1.  Personnel

Personnel will come from the shareholder population as much as possible.  UNISONIA has been designed to make use of a diverse amount of creative administrative talent which would oversee and champion the numerous emphasis areas this outline describes.

The general positive attitude of the community will foster high productivity through out the administrative personnel.

The UNI-CITI offers a full range of excellent benefits for individuals at various levels of skill and experience, from the new graduate to the experienced worker nearing retirement age.

Benefits include an outstanding retirement plan; life, health, dental and vision insurance; paid sick leave and disability benefits; and personal and vacation leave. In-house training programs and promotional opportunities for career advancement are also excellent.

> *"A different world cannot be built by indifferent people."*
> ~ **Anonymous**

## 2. Financial

UNISONIA will join with a large investment banking establishment, large insurance company and/or an other financial entity such as a mall developer to purchase land to lay out streets, water, electric, cable, and telephone lines, through a developer. The developer will construct the streams and lakes and establish the nucleus businesses and shops in the UNI-CITI CENTRE. They will also establish production facilities for such products as PYRAMOD space-frame, sandwich panel and other production facilities for other new products aiming at Telemarketing.

One third of the price of the lot will be a shareholders equity for corporate stock in the business facilities of UNISONIA. This investment will establish leveraging funds for immediate building of UNISONIA.

An investment buy-back situation will exist issuing bonds for the Citi to buy back equity.

Credit Unions are a unique financial institution which could be compatible with UNISONIA. To understand credit unions, it is necessary to look at their roots and understand the theory of cooperatives.

"A cooperative is a business voluntarily owned and controlled by its member patrons and operated for them and by them on a non-profit or cost basis. It is owned by the people who use it. It is organized and incorporated to engage in economic activities with certain ideals of democracy, social consciousness, and human relations included. A cooperative provides services and benefits for its members in proportion to the use they make of their organization, rather than earning profits for the shareholders as investors," said Marvin ASKARIS (Cooperatives, Principles and Practices).

The idea of cooperation may seem as commonplace to you as picking up your children at school on the way home from work and knowing that your spouse will stop at the grocery store to get a few things for dinner. Cooperation is part of your daily routine.

But what would happen to your peaceful co-existence with family, friends, and fellow employees if you were to shirk your responsibilities and depend on someone else to pick up the slack?

Open communication, education and positive efforts in getting everyone involved will naturally take place through each UNI-PARK Association.

Imagine trying to implement the principles of cooperation on a worldwide basis, taking into account the vast number of cultural, social, economic, religious, racial, and governmental distinctions.

Although there may be ethnic differences, the underlying values of equality, equity and mutual self-help are fundamental to any successful cooperative. Throughout history people have worked together to do collectively what could not be done individually. Self help through mutual assistance has enabled civilization to develop and grow.

- •Investment Advisors **# 105**
- •Credit Unions **# 106**

### WHEN WE BUILD

*When we build, let us think that we build forever. Let it not be for present delight nor for present use alone. Let it be such work as our descendants will thank us for, and let us think, as we lay stone on stone, that a time is to come when those stones will be held sacred because our hands have touched them, and that men will say as they look upon the labor and wrought substance of them.. "See! This our Fathers did for us."*

**~ John Ruskin**

### 3. Facilities

Two homes per day will be built making 2,500 homes in five years. The CITI CENTRE will be built to accommodate the needs of the growing community at the same time the manufacturing facilities for space frames, panels, patio deck components, other building accessories and many other production items used in a flourishing community.

## B. ECONOMIC DEVELOPMENT

Economic Development is a concern for most communities. The level of service and quality of life environment a community provides to its residents is directly effected by the quality and quantity of development. It is a continuous activity, and knowing how to manage that activity is essential. Economic Development is a job which requires many skills and a team-orientated approach.

Questions must be considered like how does a community estimate its development needs? What portion of those needs can be satisfied internally through the growth of existing business potential in the community? Which businesses have a rational economic relationship to the community and which ones have expansion plans? How should you present your community to investors? What are the public and private tools which can be used to encourage development? These are just some of the questions facing communities concerned about their future.

The many products needed in building two or more houses per day plus two sets of kitchens and bathroom cabinets; concrete and wood fence, patios and patio decks, stair units and all the other items to be manufactured will keep many people employed. Economic development will be done to a great extent from within. Other people-friendly, environment-friendly industry desiring to come in will be welcomed.

After most homes are built in the UNI-CITI, housing and production will be marketed outside the community.

The importance of a solid economic base in the community cannot be under stressed. Job opportunities must be available to provide fulfillment for the community at large.

• Economic Development **# 107**

## 1. Research, Development and Industrial Productivity

Research, development and industrial productivity are considered very important to create continued growth in employment, economic growth and Uni-citizen services. Specific research comes after the creative spark of intuition takes place, joining other sparks of ingenuity into a fire to be harnessed for good.

> *"Before the fact comes the idea."*
> ~ **Hubert H. Humphrey**

Production of such products as housing components, fencing, patio components, health food products, etc., would be advisable.

### Step Ladder Loan or Grant

R. L. White, Executive Vice President of Mobay Corporation, said in the *Plastic Trends Magazine* April 1987 that "The factors that frequently determine the ultimate fate of creative ideas are often shared by successful innovators. Among these factors are determination, independence, courage, and willingness to take risks." Along this line Holtzberg says, "Above and beyond anything else, you've got to be a good salesman to be successful at dream engineering."

Management, in White's view, must play an important role "in helping to bring out these creative characteristics in people and to provide the environment, the tools, the exchange of ideas and, most important, the freedom to work."

Every business starts with an idea, but many thousands of worthwhile ideas each year lie dormant due in part to a lack of a business plan, which every bank, venture capital source or business developer requires.

In many cases, the individual creating the idea is not able to develop a total business plan and portfolio because of a lack of funds for engineering, design, accounting, legal, clerical, and other miscellaneous expenses.

*The Dream~*
*Without a dream, you cannot make a dream come true.*

*~Author Unknown*

But this does not mean the idea is not good; it just needs a little help.

UNISONIA provides a Step Ladder Loan/Grant program to assist Inventor/ Entrepreneurs in the preliminary pay for services such as engineering, design, accounting, legal, clerical, and printing.

A 5-year, $5,000.00 loan or grant for groups or persons for developing a business plan and/or a $10,000.00 investment on the part of the Uni/Citi to provide equity in the start up of companies would be a business incubation program.

## Small Business/Inventory/Entrepreneur Initiative

Small communities of less than 10,000 people may want to look seriously at a program which would be planting seeds for immediate as well as future grass roots economic development.

Every business had a specific starting point. We need to START business in order for it to grow. The greatest number of new jobs are created by new small businesses in the U.S. We need to help make this happen in small communities as well.

Many small business development centers help put business plans together, but a package of at least the following is necessary before a realistic business plan can be *achieved*.

| | |
|---|---|
| Research and development background information compiled. | 15% |
| •Product prototype, pictures, drawings, engineering, patent search patent, copyright protection, production research | 30% |
| Preliminary accounting, costing, etc. | 10% |
| Professional illustrative printed material | 15% |
| Preliminary marketing study. | 30% |

All of this takes a great amount of effort, time and money on the part of the inventor/entrepreneur.

I believe the great job the staffs at the Small Business Development Centers are doing could be greatly enhanced, helping to create many more jobs if a program could be put into place to help inventor/entrepreneurs put together. The Rest of the Package as suggested above.

This program is a significant key to starting many new businesses which in turn could be instrumental in creating many jobs in the Uni-Citi.

Entrepreneurial production from new ideas has provided over 50% of the new jobs in the United States in recent years. We cannot afford to allow these many potential job producing opportunities to evaporate.

**Entrepreneurial Business Plan Outline**

**How to develop (write) your Business Plan and Financial Proposal**

**INTRODUCTION**

There are three main functions of any business you operate or plan to start.

1. You must produce your product or service.
2. You must market and sell your product.
3. You must finance and control your operation.

A business plan describes just how you are going to accomplish these functions and achieve a profit.

**Purpose and Use**

In writing your business plan, you should consider it fulfills three major roles for you the business owner.

♦ **Sales Tool** - The plan tells your story in a way which will get the lenders' attention, interest, and consent to finance.

♦ **Communication Tool** - The plan explains to your suppliers, distributors and employees what your business is about and how you are going to accomplish your objectives.

♦ **Management Tool** - The plan allows you to chart a course for implementing your ideas, managing your businesses progress and most importantly evaluating your assumptions.

## BUSINESS AND FINANCIAL PLAN OUTLINE

1. **Executive Summary**
   Objective-Key Points
2. **Industry and Company**
3. **Product or Service**
4. **Target Markets**
5. **Competition**
6. **Marketing Strategy**
7. **Operations**
8. **Management**
9. **Schedule of Implementation**
10. **Critical Risk and Problems**
11. **Financial Information**
   Summary of funding request - Past and Current
      YTD Financials - Financial Projections
      (BS, P & L, CF)

- Step Ladder Loans **# 108**


## 2. Purchasing

Since purchasing can obtain building materials and appliances in larger quantities, the savings will be passed on to the shareholders. Fleet purchases of vehicles may be advisable as well as other large purchases, such as computers and appliances.

Leasing of cars, appliances, furniture, and boats, to the Uni-Citizens if they choose.
  •Buyer's Clubs. **# 109**

PROXIMA DATA DISPLAY 1-800-US-MISCO

## 3. Marketing

UNISONIA will attract the interest of people world wide because of the way it addresses the needs of individuals and families in this day and time. The concept will be promoted and offered to all who would desire being a productive part in an affordable contemporary community.

The Marketing Department of the Uni-Citi Corporation will be actively involved in helping to sell all products produced in conjunction with the Uni-Citi.

## 4. UNI-QUAD/PARK Coordination

A representative from each of the seven UNI-PARKS within each Uni-Quad will coordinate activities within the Uni-Quad and will also serve on the UNI-CITI Executive Advisory Board.

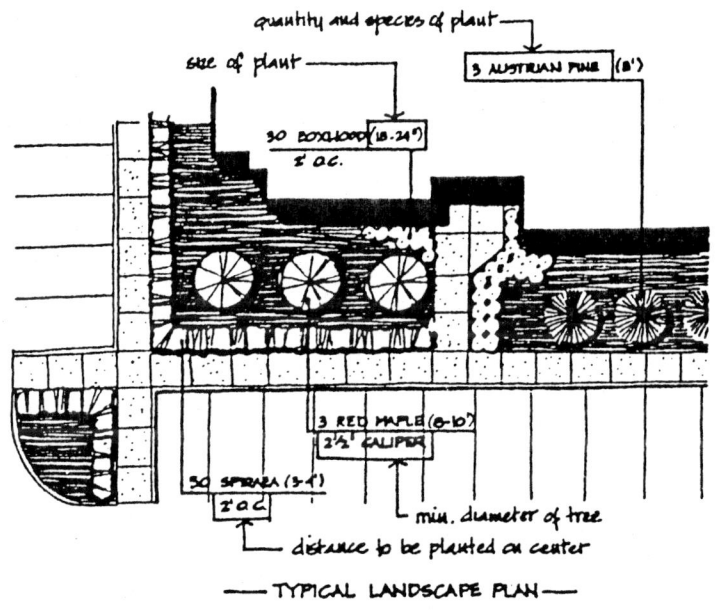

— TYPICAL LANDSCAPE PLAN —

## Service Park

The Service Park will immediately begin its activity with the auto service area, nature trails, any industrial development, clinic, spiritual center, or other compatible service organizations, including golf course and other recreational facilities.

## 5. UNI-CENTRE

The UNI-CENTRE will be started in the early stages of UNISONIA. This will create employment for the Shareholders.

169

Retail stores and shops will provide all necessary goods and services that a well rounded community needs.

The New Store concept provides small cities with up scale goods -- the prototype for a new kind of department store designed for smaller cities is created to give the feel of an affluent shopping center inside one store. The centre will provide upscale goods to consumers who live in areas that can't lure many department store giants. The unit will have the cohesive look of a department store but individual store sections, such as shoes or men's wear, will be leased to private operators.

"The centre will be like a Marshall Field's, only smaller. The interior image will say 'department store' because no dividing walls are planned. Each 5,000 square-foot department will bear a subtitle name that identifies it with the exclusive retailer of that section," said the development coordinator for the concept.

A staff design consultant will be available to occupants. The designer may not be used by every retailer but will coordinate the different sections' displays to guarantee the consistency of the overall look.

Nearly 90 percent of the centre will be filled by local merchants, with one or two national retailers in the remaining space. The 30,000 square-foot store will devote at least 10,000 feet to apparel. Ten to 15 additional tenants are sought to offer other department store goods, such as furniture, housewares and jewelry.

Pricing equity and competition will be determined by the corporate offices and management of the UNI-CITI together with the individual store owners in a fair manner.

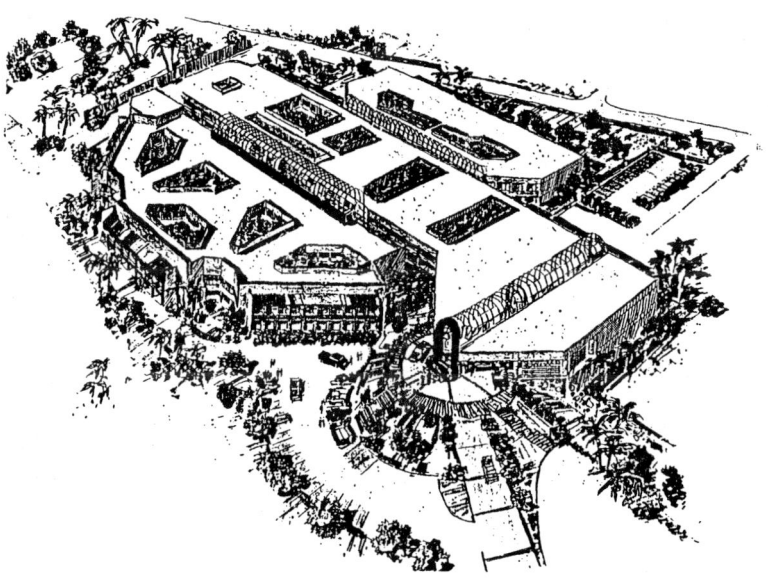

Demensions - Illustration by Robert Hanncock

A home improvement products retailer will be offered this section in a boutique setting of about 500 to 1,000 square feet. It would be a department where customers could purchase decorative hardware, bath and kitchen furnishings and other hard-to-find merchandise as well as the common every day wares.

Without much space for the prospective home improvement department, the section could be run like a catalog showroom for the centre's varied customers.

The facility will anchor a 100-acre complex that includes a

health club, grocery store and bank. The multi-million dollar building will have separate entrances on each of two levels. A glass enclosed courtyard will add light, while brass, chrome and marble will create the shopping environment the customer desires.

The centre plans to provide all the amenities a shopping mall would have, including display services, advertising and security. A Uni-Citi credit card is also a possibility.

•The Developer **# 110**

The Uni-Centre, which could also include a meeting/convention center, may be built in the shape of a donut four or five stories high with the open area in the center being a covered mall. A column projecting up the center could support a tipi-style, flexible covering for the landscaped mall, and could also facilitate a people carrier to the top of a twelve-story high column with observatory. The Centre could include art galleries, museums, dance studios, and library.


## UNIQUAD Park

Administratively, all seven Uni-Parks (unless otherwise dictated by the terrain) have a representative on the managing board of the approximate 25-acre park in the center of their Uniquad, 1/4th of residential portion of the community.

**Service Park**

The Service Park is intended to serve the needs of the Unisonians in numerous ways:

1. Health offices and clinics.

2. Business and production facilities.

3. Religious organizations using joint-use facilities together with business and production facilities. Parking may also be joint-use resources.

4. Vehicle service facilities.

5. Protected vehicle storage parking.

6. Golf course, volleyball courts and trails.

7. Memorial gardens.

8. Outdoor concert and arts facilities.

9.  Miscellaneous sports facilities.

10. Motel/hotel meeting facilities.

Eight advisory board member representatives advise the corporate Uni-citi governing board relative to positive and productive service park business management.

## Commercial Facility Design Service

Professional space and facility planners, architects, designers, and other consultants will be available for any entrepreneur/small business persons requesting such assistance in developing their business plan.

## 6. Realty Service

The Realty Service Division of the corporation will coordinate sale of lots and work in close proximity with administration, including valuation enhancement recommendations to property owners' associations.

•National Association of Realtors # 111

## C. PLANNING

The planning processes are a constantly updating endeavor and every effort to creatively develop people-oriented growth potential for all Uni-citizens is always taking place.

Every aspect of Unisonian life will constantly be reviewed, planned and developed, toward non entropy.

## 1. Structures and Facilities Design

Structures and facilities will be designed through the administrative office of planning with the assistance of computer aided design systems, the purpose of which would be to provide maximum useability, economy and practical space use while having pleasing aesthetic input by staff and consultant designers.

Administration will conduct the human potential, environmental land use, through positive communications, achieving a successful community beyond comprehension.

I sincerely appreciate the solid research and basic realism the Science Council of Canada has done in *CITIES FOR TOMORROW.* It is so relevant to our times and to UNISONIA - to Our Future. I did not want it to get lost - it is far too important not to be available for public study. I have edited it as follows, (see Appendix I.)

Following also are summaries of articles from *Industrial Design Magazine* by George Nelson (see Appendix II), and Lawrence Halprin (see Appendix III.).

Ivan L. Loesch

## APPENDIX I

## CITIES FOR TOMORROW
(out of print)

## SCIENCE COUNCIL OF CANADA

Minister of Supply and Service CANADA (copyright)
Catalog No, 5522-1971-14
Ottawa, Canada K1A os9

O. M. Solandt, Chairman of the Science Council of Canada in his presentation of the full report (of which these are excerpts) to the Right Honorable Pierre Elliot Trudeau P.C.,M.P. Prime Minister of Canada.

You will find the thread of human values is woven throughout this report. Although we early gave up the attempt of a frontal attach on quality of environment, an ecological preoccupational pervades our whole study.

The Science Council Committee, composed as it was of experts whose centres of operation were esthetic, social, economic and political, as well as technical and scientific, was at some pains to keep this historical perspective in view and to achieve a minimum consensus on the relative weight of the issues. It was tempted to concentrate its thinking on the future and to project the whole urban problem upon the "New City." But this prospect was abandoned for the good reason that it threatened an over-extension of the joint competence of its members and the very mission of the Science Council itself. Although utopia is no longer a derisive term and, indeed, futurism is fashionable, we chose to adhere more closely to the realities of the day.

It was felt that the generalist's (or "totalist's") approach would be satisfied by a recommendation for a permanent study. We were able only to outline the design of this study, where "everything relates to everything" (it is tempting to say this with an Irish accent). This frustration of the engineer and of the planner should be the ecologist's challenge. And so it is. The identification of all significant parameters is the ecologist's detective job. This first step is one of great magnitude and it turned out that our Committee could not undertake it. For this reason, the idea of "a major program" was abandoned by the Science Council Committee.

I hope we have not succumbed to the naivete' of compulsive sophistication by putting our faith in system analysis. However, at a time when musicians and biblical scholars are learning to test their powers of perception by seeking the help of computers, maybe scientists and technologists are not too far out in their "great expectations." There are many apprentice-sorcerers among us, and the presumption of some of the high priests of gadgetry can still do a great deal of harm. But surely it is the scientist's mission to use more and better technology, not less.

To use it well, and place man at the centre, is also our responsibility. As scientists we bear some guilt for not having reached out to the human predicament by devising better tools for apprehending yearnings, suffering, cultural and personal imagery, and other pressures that mold society as much as thirst, hunger and sexual drive. The urging of Jeremy Bentham, no less than the enlightenment of Charles Darwin and his twentieth century disciples, should have led us earlier to a better synthesis of research and development through the pursuit of a more lucid motivation and a better-controlled technological and economic instrumentation.

It should give the scientific community singular pride if it were capable of persuading the various levels of government to adopt our first two resolutions and set the co-ordinated manpower required to the business of recording, forecasting and planning the design, the re-shaping and the development of our urban environment. This is a redoubtable assignment...Can we achieve the proposed goals within the present socio-economic system as it stands? I think we cannot, but I see many signs of the coming acceptance of a more austere (less consumer-oriented) way of life. The emerging new ethic, if it has placed man in the centre, has also displaced the value of individual salvation with that of collective salvation.

This greater preoccupation with participation and with the variety inherent in human relationships offers the strongest possible bolster to the planning of the environment, to the place of living as well as to the style of living. A new balance between economic and spatial design begs to be achieved.

Thus diversity and choice become the key words in the modest contribution to urban development. Transportation, housing, recycling of waste and communications between citizen and government are tied together by these central preoccupations. Freedom to live and to work in congenial habitats with congenial people is now the lot of the "happy few." Unregulated urban transportation, poor housing opportunities, the obnoxiousness of pollution and waste disposal, as well as faulty information are concerning the city-dweller into growing frustration at this high tide of national wealth. We have tried to probe some of the neuralgic points of the related crises in the urban anatomy. We are bound to conclude that the best thinking of the scientists and the full knowledge and skill of our technologists will continue to misfire if we find no better way of encompassing the urban environment as a whole, and if our national purposes cannot be more clearly geared to a goal higher than mere economic growth.

Pierre Dansereau, Chairman, Committee on Urban Development

Science Council of Canada

Dr. Dirk Maasland, Dr. W. L. Sauer, Dr. Saul N. Silverman

## APPENDIX II

## THE HUMAN FACTORS by George Nelson
*Industrial Design Magazine*

"DESIGN MUST ENHANCE THE QUALITY OF LIFE" AND "THE HUMANE DESIGNER" are both articles authored by George Nelson, president of George Nelson and Company and the American partner in the British firm, Pentagram Design, in New York.

Both articles were published in *Industrial Design Magazine*.

Designers are obligated to study their own values and to question what they're told, argues this designer and writer. His contentions are excerpted from the chapter titled Design and Human Needs in "George Nelson on Design," which The Whitney Library of Design published. In midtown Manhattan, between 6th and 7th Avenues, there is a kind of minipark that cuts through the block between 48th and 49th. It contains benches, planting, a tunnel of clear plastic that penetrates a waterfall. My 18-year-old son and I used it as a shortcut on a quick shopping excursion and he was impressed. "If all of New York was designed like this," he observed, "it would be a terrific place." Why aren't cities designed for people? Why indeed?

One reason an intelligent teenager can ask questions like this today is that so many cities are clearly not designed for people at all, and it is beginning to show; another reason is that such questions concern the young more than they did a few years back, and they may be taken as a reaction to the general decline in the quality of life throughout the society.

The voices raised with such questions as my son's, the slowly increasing concern with values generally ignored, are part of a large and radical social transformation and they eventually effect the work of the designer. According to these new attitudes, he must be dedicated to serving human needs.

It is a noble aim, this idea of a career dedicated to the service of others, and we could do worse than spend time examining it, for it turns out to be less easy than it sounds. It calls for greater sensitivity than we commonly display, and it requires a great deal more homework than we are accustomed to devote to such matters. Part of the problem lies in brainwashing to which we have been subjected to since babyhood: as a society we have little or no interest in human needs and in consequence we know almost nothing about them. What we believe in is the expert, specialists control of situations. 'Give us the problem and we will hand you the solution.'

Design for human needs has to deal with psychological responses and these have to do with our senses rather than our minds. This is surprisingly difficult for members of a society conditioned to believe that the logic of science answers all questions and that the methods of technology can cope with anything. We are learning from the lumps on our heads that this simply is not so.

For designers of things and spaces in an advanced industrial society at this time it appears that what we call human needs are more likely to be met through an understanding of the sensory, non-rational elements than by more technology. Anyone who has traveled abroad knows that the older cities, built with a more primitive technology, are more "humane" than modern ones, and if we analyze some of the differences, we find...that the old cities give more exercise, so to speak, to our senses and that the sequences of visual experience are richer than in modern cities.

As a society, we have been remarkably indifferent to people generally. Ordinarily we do not notice the evidence, but it is everywhere. In any but a tiny sampling of airports we can note that luggage and supplies are handled with tender care while passengers are left to drag themselves through mile-long corridors. Most housing for the poor is so poorly conceived, so destructive of the occupants' dignity and vitality, that it creates more problems than it solves.

The most stubborn obstacles to humane design are our dominant social values, which have conditioned us to believe in the essential worthlessness and expendability of people. One reason we believe this is that so much has been done to make people worthless and expendable...

The present concern with human needs is, like so many other manifestations of the present time, a grassroots movement. It is not organized. The ideas no longer come down from the top but spring up in random fashion.

Political action does not necessarily involve adherence to one or another of the dominant ideologies, nor does it demand membership in a party. It is particularly true in this case, for the issues do not define themselves in terms of a struggle for power, but rather as a search for life.

This search is going on at many levels all over the world. It ranges from a simple desire to keep the bombs from leaving their silos to a struggle for more habitable environments. In the eyes of political prisoners or people without food this might seem very far removed from the realities of existence, but they are all part of the same thing. Since all political parties claim to be pro-people, and none shows the slightest interest in the quality of life, people involved in such a search tend to be individuals or small groups.

## Will the Act Enhance Life?

It is our fate, recalling the ancient Chinese curse, to live in interesting times. The heads of everyone of us are full of lumps from these interesting times and anyone may be forgiven for finding himself in a state of confusion about practically anything one can name.

Still, there is one way to simplify an impossibly complicated situation which I find both practical and comforting. It is to look at whatever one is doing and to decide whether it is an act that will enhance life, even to the most minute degree, or something that will work against life.

## The Humane Designer

It is a truism to observe that there is constant interaction between people and environments. A clean city is produced by clean people; it is no doubt equally true that a clean city tends to produce clean people. Like the chicken-egg example, it serves no purpose to argue which comes first. There is a dynamic interaction, always building up or running down.

There are some examples, generally involving nature in which the surrounding is dominant. People who live in very large environments (sailors, fliers, ranchers) are physically different from people who live in constricted spaces. Their eyes are different, their movements are different, the ways in which they speak are different. Mountain people can be distinguished from people of the plains. People who live in very big countries such as Brazil, Russia or the United States, do not think or react in exactly the same ways as people who have grown up on tight islands like Japan and England.

But whenever the environment is manmade, whatever its size, we are led to think about interactions, rather than simple, direct influence or conditioning. Consider the endless arguments about slums. How many times have we heard the argument that slums create slum people? About the same number of times, I would guess, that we have been told that slum people create slums. About the only thing on which there is agreement is that the two coexist.

Wherever there is an artifact, whether a small object or an entire synthetic environment, there has to be a designer. It does not matter whether the "designer" is an individual or a group, and it matters even less what the designer calls himself. Baron Haussmann is always thought of as the man who designed modern Paris, although he was not a designer in the professional sense, and the same was true of Robert Moses in his heyday, when he was building the first parkways out of New York City.

In all cases when objects, small or large, are built there is inevitably a designer, for the simple reason that nothing can be built until there is a design or plan for it. Even a child making a sand castle has some kind of picture in mind while making it. The fact that in such instances there is a good bit of improvisation simply means that the picture, or design, emerges only a split second before making begins. It has to be there.

Definitions of the designer vary enormously with time and place. In the advanced industrial societies, "designer" tends to mean "industrial designer" because most things are made within an industrial framework. But, there are times and places which have no such framework, and in such instances, the word means something else. Architects are designers whose work has traditionally been confined to buildings, although these limitations are now changing. Physicists are designers when they conceive and build devices to check out an hypothesis. Iron foundry foremen are designers when they decide on the surface pattern of a manhole cover.

For argument's sake, let's consider the designer to be an individual or a group which, when presented with a problem to be solved, comes up with an answer which has a visible shape or form. This answer always has several aspects; it has functional attributes -- that is, it works. It has a technological base. It has aesthetic qualities which cannot easily be detached from function or technology, but which are not the same as either. It also has a social meaning.

Nobody builds cathedrals or rockets without some belief in whatever these objects stand for. Occasionally, this social meaning expands to achieve a powerful impact. Such subjects as the Eiffel Tower, the Woolworth Building and the Brooklyn Bridge had enormous influence on the thinking and the vision of the societies which produced them. Sometime the influence is so strong that the effects are political, with consequent changes in the course of history. Such examples are especially common in the area of military activity.

### Design in War and Peace

In 53 B.C., Marcus Cassius, Roman Proconsul of Syria, invaded Parthia with 40,000 men and the general idea of extending the Empire as far as India. The result was total disaster, largely because of the design of the Parthian bow, a weapon built like a laminated spring, with such range and power that the Roman Legions were helpless against it. The body count, if you will excuse the expression, was 20,000 dead and 10,000 prisoners, not because the Parthians had a better general, but because they had a better designer.

While military history offers spectacular examples of the influence of design, there is plenty of evidence of the influence of the designer in any number of peacetime activities. Consider, for instance, the popular image of big-city people as nervous, pressured, harassed by crowding, noise and work. One of the most important basis for this myth is the design of city streets.

A city street consists of a roadway flanked by sidewalks which, in turn, are bounded by buildings. The cars, crushed together like armored beetles in passages too narrow for them, offer the pedestrian no chance to cross the roadway without danger to life and limb. One response to this problem, a palliative rather than a solution, is the traffic light, a device which can only function on a rhythmic basis--so many seconds for "go" and so many for "stop." This has led to a new and powerful disciplining of urban populations: a vast urban pattern of leaps and stops comes into existence, with both drivers and pedestrians conditioned to watch the lights anxiously and to spring forward on green.

One result of the stop-and-go pattern of pedestrian movement is the end of pleasurable strolling, a development in individual behavior which is reinforced by the design of sidewalks. A sidewalk in the modern city is a narrow band of some hard material which is bounded on one side by the curb, which is crowded by parked or moving cars, and on the other by the hard fronts of buildings. Furthermore, if the pedestrians do not form themselves into right and left lanes like the cars, no movement at all is possible during rush periods. Window shopping, one of the pleasures of walking in cities, thus becomes extremely difficult.

Thus, we get a picture of the modern individual interacting with an anti- human environment, with frustration and irritation as the chief byproduct. One has only to think of walks in the country, or in parks, or shopping malls or in pizzas of old cities to see how destructive the interaction between street design and people can be. The one comfort we can always extract from such examples is that they are useful in indicating the directions for change. Here I can give you a personal example.

In 1943, I found myself looking through a pile of 8x10 glossy photographs, air views of the centers of cities in the 150,000 to 250,000 range. I have forgotten why I was doing this, but what I do remember was being struck by the absolutely uniform ring of blight around all of the downtown business districts.

This decayed ring was made up of structures which had surrounded the original town or village center, consisting of large houses, churches and municipal elements such as fire and police stations. With the passage of time the center had grown, driving out residential and other uses, but it had not grown, driving out residential and other uses, but it had not grown enough to take over the ring. As a result, marginal uses such as rooming houses, gas stations and cheap laundries had come in, leading to further decay in both the ring as a neighborhood and in the structures.

Suddenly, it occurred to me that this decay might be viewed as organic, and I began scaling off distances within the ring. I found that the entire area inside was walkable--lengths were on the order of five to eight blocks, and widths were less. In the forties we were already aware of the problems being created by the motor car, and the idea of an undisturbed downtown pedestrian area was attractive. Furthermore, the presidential campaign which involved Herbert Hoover and Franklin Roosevelt was fresh in our minds. It was during this campaign that Mr. Hoover had predicted that if his opponent was elected, grass would presently be growing in Times Square. As a New Yorker, I was captivated by visions of a Times Square where cows could graze, and I voted for Roosevelt.

Excited by the vision of grass growing within an entire downtown area, I developed a project based on the center of Bridgeport, Connecticut, and named it "Grass on Main Street."

Thanks to an industrial sponsor, the project was published in the *Saturday Evening Post,* and the pedestrian mall came into theoretical existence as a new urban element (in the 20th century context).

The proposal, back in 1943, aroused no interest whatever. As I recall, of the six or eight million readers the post claimed to reach each week, there was exactly one letter. Within a dozen years, however, the first of such malls began to appear and today, of course, no city would consider itself up-to-date without some areas from which cars are excluded. The social impact of such proposals and projects is, of course, considerable, for it changes the vision of the city from a haphazard assembly of artifacts to that of a community in which planning for human needs begins to receive attention.

## Design as a Powerful Tool

The great bulk of significant design today has to do with those points where the greatest social stress is felt, and this is within the cities, or rather within those metropolitan regions where cities and suburbs are coalescing into corridors of huge dimensions.

I am not suggesting that design can "cure" the ills which accompany massive social transformations, but rather that the evolution of design is an important part of a process of interaction in which people and environments affect each other. I am suggesting that design is an important part of a process of interaction in which people and environments affect each other. I am suggesting that design, in reflecting social change, can be used as a very powerful tool in accelerating those changes which appear to be desirable.

The process is complex, especially at a time when established materialistic values are being attached on all sides, but the fact that the elements in such conflicts are a confusing mix of political, racial, economic and philosophical elements does not rule out the very real possibilities for design to act as a catalytic agent for constructive change.

There is an interesting illustration of this on Manhattan Island right now. A few years ago the city was given its first "minipark" by William Paley, chairman of the board of CBS. The park is located in the mid-50's, on fantastically expensive property and consists of brick walls, a waterfall, a few trees and some tables and chairs on perhaps 8,000 square foot of ground. It is reputed to have cost $2.5 million and has been enthusiastically used by thousands. Mr. Paley earned the well-deserved reputation of a public benefactor. Less publicized are some of the events which followed, which include a veritable rash of miniparks.

Builders who want to put up high buildings in New York are subject to zoning ordinances, and one of the tools with which they can work is their rights on undeveloped property. In other words, a 50-story building can only be built if some land is left free, and this is resulting in the rapid emergence of vestpocket parks in conjunction with the buildings. The interesting thing about these parks is that they are being designed with great care and built at great expense by individuals and syndicates concerned only (so the myth goes) with return on investment and profit. Why are they doing it? The law requires that certain pieces of land be left undeveloped. Iit does not stipulate the owners install fountains, seating, outdoor cafes, and other amenities.

What is happening, I think, is that design has again acted as a prod to both public and private consciences and the vision of the mega-city is being changed as a result. Large building owners have that these amenities are an assist in getting tenants, but I do not believe that the motivation is entirely commercial. It seems far more likely that a new kind of emulation is going on, stimulated by the demonstration provided by Paley Park, with a new role for the entrepreneur as a leader in community beautification. His status as a citizen is coming to depend on how well he plays out this role.

The kinds of projects I have been describing are created by an unpredictable mix of designers and of men at the center of political and financial power. Traditionally the designer, like the artist, has always been a servant to the rulers. Today his responsibilities and his potential are greater, for his client, more often than not, belongs to a large group of functionally blind. This is not the result of natural causes, but rather the outcome of a carefully calculated method of education.

This concept of a specific disability of modern man is by no means my own; there is an entire literature on the subject. The only point we need deal with is its meaning, which has to take into account its origin.

In pre-technological societies, before the Industrial Revolution, the processes of making, design, sales, and consumption were relatively integrated. Every child knew how wagons were built, horses shod, crops harvested, flour milled, houses built, and so on. The fragmentation of thinking and feeling began with the fragmentation of work in factories. The worker ceased to make things and became someone who performed piecemeal operations. This process of fragmentation led to the fragmentation of the citizen who became a proletarian; the alienation of the worker from his work presently appeared as the alienation of the individual.

The process of education was used to assist in these developments. A technological society needs people who can read and write, add and subtract and perform piecemeal tasks. It does not need individuals who can see or feel. Thus the schools, whose task is always to prepare individuals for life in the larger society, developed their curricula to take care of these needs and to ignore other aspects of human development not needed by business and industry.

## Decay of the City

Along with all this, the sources of visual variety and excitement dried up, leaving little in the cities but slums and monuments to commerce and industry. Even the upper classes, which during the Age of Enlightenment and earlier had prided themselves on their sophistication with regard to architecture, urban design, painting and sculpture, sent their children to schools where the studies were confined to languages, history and sciences. Today's elites plus the vast middle classes are not much better off.

A Thomas Jefferson was equipped to design his own house or university if he felt like it; his upbringing as an 18th century gentleman included this kind of training. A Pericles was able to talk to a Phidias or an Iktinos in their own language. This situation does not repeat itself in the case of modern captains of industry, although every statement has its own exceptions, and in twenty-five years of working with business and industry I have encountered two, perhaps three visually sophisticated clients.

What this means in practical terms, of course, is that given a wish to ornament a community, on the part of a man with public or private power, he cannot function without someone who can show him how to turn this vague dream into something palpable and visible. Thus, the designer becomes the seeing individual with the unique power and responsibility to come up with something that will gratify the sponsor and favorably impress his public. All too often, to be sure, what happens is a pageant in which the blind lead the blind, but wherever anything ennobling, or even positive happens in the modern landscape, there is a designer of talent and sensibility behind it. Thus, we come, not for the first time in history, to the paradox of the servant with more real power, ultimately, than his master.

There is something on top of all of this which gives today's designer his truly astonishing potential: this is the depth of the craving--now shared by a vast majority of the population--for humane environments.

Societies, like individuals, seem to do their most effective learning from the lumps on their heads, and we have had our full share in the past few decades. Whether the issue be pollution, or fallout, urban crime or violence, or municipal insolvency, the lessons now being pondered have to do with the abrupt shift of technology from a blessing to a poison, along with the shocking discovery that affluence does not automatically provide the "good life" and the questions so urgently being asked by a generation of children who were encouraged to think for themselves.

The real heritage of the period of science and invention is the confidence that we can alter the physical environment to suit our purpose and with this there is the painful knowledge that these alterations all carry a price tag. The outcome is a new awareness of the responsibilities that go with power, and a shift of values that says, in effect, that the only legitimate use of power is for the enhancement of the human existence.

The utopia implied by these brave words is somewhere over the visible horizon. But the awareness is here now.

We have achieved sobriety of a kind, if not maturity. New social goals, beginning to make sense, arouse the loyalties and release the energies of the population.

The response of the designer to such changes is to search for new forms which, when visible to the public, will make the nature of the change comprehensible. The public, in looking at these new statements about new realities, may again begin to see its environment as a totality affecting the quality of life.

One final example of the designer as a social catalyst, again from personal experience, has to do with a private search for a new form within the urban landscape, and the motivations for the search.

The search has to do with a series of private observations, which led to the conviction that the major source of visual pollution in cities is not billboards, gas stations and telephone wires, undesirable as these may be, but buildings. In any number of cities, the unending succession of buildings and streets is an affront to the eyes and a burden on the spirit. I am not talking about good or bad buildings, but simply of the overwhelming quantity of hard-edged structures which offer no relief to the inhabitant.

Since buildings exist in vast numbers in cities because there is a need for them, one way to tackle the problems created by sheer bulk is to make the buildings invisible. This may sound like a contradiction in terms, but if we examine the mix of structures in the modern city, we find that many types are windowless: warehouses, telephone exchanges, department stores and shops of all kinds, parking garages, movie theaters, auditoriums and so on. All such services can be clustered within synthetic hills, creating the interesting possibility of urban elements which are full of life and activity inside, while the outer skin of planted earth and terraces may be used as a public amenity, and serve visually as a new element in the city scape; soft rather that hard, green instead of gray, relaxed rather than tense.

Such elements are both feasible and overdue: they could be built where needed at a very large scale, contain streets and parking, become a powerful tool for conserving energy, and restore to the city what it so urgently needs--a sense of rhythm and open space.

In this example, the design was triggered, not by the demands of a client, but by speculation about some of the real needs of the city and the preliminary research work done by my class at the Graduate School of Design at Harvard.

Since our society, oddly enough, has little or no interest in experimental building, the schools are the only place where it can be carried on. With any luck at all, the results will be clear enough to be presented to wider publics and once again, the designer's efforts to sustain a constructive role will be tested by professional criticism and by public response. If this venture should be successful, the present vision of the options open to the modern city will be enriched, and the designer's role as social catalyst will be further solidified.

All of our past training and experience, whether as architects, industrial and graphic designers, as landscape architects, urban or interior designers, has been leading us, I think, to an awareness that the role of design has been expanding steadily in both scope and significance; that we are now confronting the real jackpot design questions of our time, which are largely at the urban level. The very nature of these problems makes interdisciplinary activity essential, and this, in turn, will reinforce the designer's capability to deal with his larger responsibility, which is to function as a responsive and effective agent during a time of change.

## APPENDIX III

## "THE HUMANE CITY" by Lawrence Halprin
### *Industrial Design Magazine*

The "planned city" must be planned so that people are not as Lawrence Halprin says, "dragooned into some planners or government officials preconceived notion of what is good for them."

I want people to feel the vibrance, the creativity, and vitality, much of which can be experienced in smaller communities if people are open to and allow a creative attitude and motivation to flow in an innovatively conceived smaller community.

The "Sense of Community" means communication, fellowship, caring, working for common goals, common wealth, open enjoyment and appreciation of other peoples capabilities, talents, desires, needs, and feelings.

Lawrence Halprin has included so much valuable information, with such understandable feeling, I wanted his writing available for you to read. It is an important work.

## THE HUMANE CITY

By Lawrence Halprin, President
Lawrence Halprin and Associates
Reprinted from *Industrial Design Magazine*

I am a city man; I was born in New York and grew to young manhood there. I went to school in Cambridge and Boston. My offices are in San Francisco and New York. I have done work in Caracas, Jerusalem, Fort Worth, Portland, Berlin, Washington, D.C., Minneapolis, Chicago, San Francisco, New York--all cities with the unique characteristics that distinguish one metropolis from another, and all with that special quality that always gives me a thrill: "This is a City!"

Why does the city thrill me so? I began as a landscape architect. I am rapturously in love with nature. I am dedicated to the proper ecological relationships between manmade and nature-wrought environments. I draw life-giving and creative sustenance from the Pacific Ocean, the High Sierra, the redwood and eucalyptus groves that surround where I live. But, when I want to have creative interchange with other people; when I want to share life with others and become involved with the ongoing synergistic relationships that make a vital human environment--then I must be in the city, for that is where I find the energy, the vibrance, the vitality that denotes the community of man.

Cities have always had these meanings for men. As in Rome, the city acted as the forum where men communicated with one another, where art and culture and government and commerce and industry and religion were born and sustained.

You cannot name an important culture that did not nor does

not get its major impetus from its cities. Just think of Babylon, Athens, Sparta, Venice, Rome, Peking, Tokyo, Sidney, Rio de Janeiro, New York--the list is endless in both time and place.

But today, some of our cities are losing steam. They are becoming the nine-to-five receptacles for people engaged in just a few interests and a few occupations. For more than half of their diurnal lives, these cities are echoing wastelands, deserted by all but the people who cannot afford to leave them and those who may be transients for a few days or nights. The life is gone; the variety is fled; the motivations for people to live in and use their cities have diminished. Has this been necessary? Is there no other way for Americans to enjoy their cities, to profit from them culturally and emotionally, as well as economically? Must the veins of the city always be cut to transfuse its life's blood to the outskirts, to the two-dimensional spread that more and more surrounds all our cities? Must the less well-advantaged always be left with a declining environment in the inner city to live in, to become angry in, to be trapped and impotent in? How can men have a say about these things? How can they be a force in determining what their cities mean and how they will change for the better.

I'll say more about this thrust toward participatory planning in a moment. First, though, let me just dwell on the idea of cities--what makes them unique; what makes one different from another.

It seems to me that all of the cities I have been in that are full of vitality still have a life around the clock, are the ones that are still lived in. Mexico City, Caracas, Paris, Rome, San Francisco, New York, New Orleans-these places are populated twenty-four hours a day; they are imbued with the vivaciousness and variety that come from many people of many backgrounds and many interests living together. There are opportunities for choice and alternative life styles. People are not regimented and dragooned into some planner's or government official's preconceived notion of "What is good for them."

True, these days in some places such as New York, there is a negative concomitant to life in the city. Many people are fearful and feel in the grip of a hostile environment that I think is the fault of people in charge for not dealing sensitively and creatively with long-term objectives for the city instead of spending all their energies and cash on short-term, stop-gap solutions to immediate problems; and, in addition, not including the people affected in the problem-solving and decision-making processes for the future.

**The Culture Of Cities**

Even in those cities where your hotel clerk -- according to current math -- cautions you not to go out into the street after sundown. There is a life of the streets. There is an intermix of attitudes and cultures and wants and needs. There is, in short, life. How different from most of our sedate and manicured suburbs. How much in contrast to some of our beautifully designed new towns! People in cities have feet, and they use them to go to the park with a girl and a bottle of wine and cheese and bread, to get to public transit, to go longer distances, to stroll along the avenues window-shopping, buying books, food, stopping in a cafe for coffee and conversation, perhaps for hitting the "body-shop bars" in the evening for a little more physically-oriented relaxation!

This all adds up to the culture of cities. In my terms "Culture of Cities" is the life, the atmosphere, the environment if you will that its people give to it. It is not the culture of the museums or the opera house or the theater; it is the people and the ways they use the city, and the things that have been provided for them to use with joy--the plazas, fountains, streets, alleys, sidewalks, arcades, public art, parks, playgrounds, meeting places, public entertainment, festivals, parades, pageants, rehabilitated older buildings, shopping precincts. These are the designed elements that can contribute--that is, allow people to live fulfilled lives in the city.

All of this speaks toward a salient requirement: cities must be various; they must have more than one life simultaneously; they cannot be a repository for commerce only and expect to function adequately for the people. Take a look at an all new part of New York: Sixth Avenue (Avenue of the Americas) between 57th Street and about 45th Street. Just a few years ago this was a varied, lively, colorful, if somewhat funky neighborhood. Small shops and enterprises lined both sides of the avenue; people strolled along it and shopped, drank and ate at all hours of the day and night. More recently, all of these little pieces of the city's life have been wiped out, obliterated, and replaced by a solemn double row of concrete and marble effigies to commerce lining the avenue. In front of each tombstone is a barren and windswept plaza, perhaps dotted by bits of sculpture. At street level, there is nothing but lobbies and branch banks--there is not one provision for anything else for anyone walking on the avenue to do. It is inhumane; it is an urban death in life.

202

The people who built this environment are not brutes, not most of them any way. I don't think they deliberately set out to offend and degrade their fellow men by erecting such a pitiless environment. The trouble was that they thought superlinearly; they only sought to build up real estate, to build containers for corporate enterprises. No other motive, no other urban objective came into the creative equation at any time. And, needless to say, the ultimate user of the environment---the people of New York---had about as much to say about what went on as you do about how a space shot is coordinated.

How does one deal with this kind of situation? How to begin to give people opportunities for making input to the changes in their cities to relieve tensions, frustrations, and anger that have been built up through their everlasting exclusion from the urban creative process of involvement of people in planning their environments, and have been successful in utilizing it in a number of cities, including Fort Worth, Tulsa, Indianapolis, and Everett, Washington. We are currently conducting what we call Take Part Workshops with the people of Harlem in New York, Charlottesville, Virginia; and we expect to perform similar services in Cleveland, Milwaukee, and Kansas City if present plans work out. What are these Take Part Workshops? In response to requests for information about them, we wrote a little book called TAKE PART. A description from it reads: "Take Part Workshops are modern versions of the New England town meeting and the old Indian pow-wow---new ways of discovering and talking with each other about what they want their city and their lives to be like. We call this 'common language' for people to use in problem-solving and decision-making together. By doing this with their elected representatives and professional consultants, people can make participation into processes demonstrating to everyone how environment can adapt to the needs of the people."

We have found in the past that people participate in their cities on at least two levels: using it and making decisions about it.

## Inviting Involvement

Participating in a city through using it means that people use their urban environment in many ways and at many times of day and night. The urban planner and designer can help them in this use/participation through creating things in the environment that will invite the involvement of people instead of being restricted in use (as is unfortunately true with the Sixth Avenue office buildings) or something that is merely an object in the urban scene for people to admire, such as a piece of sculpture. Recycled old buildings (Ghiradelli), revitalized downtown streets (Nicolett Mall), rediscovered waterfronts (Trinity River), new open spaces networks in redeveloped urban areas (Portland), and new multi uses infused into a city fabric (Yerba Buena Center) can all contribute to this involvement and the consequent quickening of life in the city.

Participating in a city through making decisions about it is also to the health of the urban body. This is what we have used Take Part Workshops for---to begin sharing and discovering processes with people from all walks of life and permit them to discover ways in which they can be instrumental in making their desires for their cities positive parts of planning for the future. Communications is a very important aspect of this. Workshops or the discoveries of workshops must be brought before the whole community on TV and through the press so that knowledge and process can be shared. Other communications techniques must make visible to the citizens how the city works. My friend Rick Wurman in Philadelphia is devoting much of his time to investigating ways of getting this vital information to people undisguised by planning jargonese or public relationese.

Finally, these two levels of participation in the city do not operate independently. Far from it. The one can lead into and infuse the other. Take Part Workshop participants can decide that what their city really needs is an open space network or a cultural center or a new medical facility. Then they can rely on their architects and planners to create those things, with ongoing involvement of the public in deciding if what is created is what they want. A place that has involved many people in the qualities of their city--fountain, park or whatever--can act as the spark that gets people to realize that they want more participation in their urban processes and to begin to investigate ways to bring about that participation.

This is the image I would like to leave you with. It implies a twenty-four hour life of the city---people living and working and playing there together, a commitment to high quality of urban environment continually upgraded in all parts and, very importantly, a variety of ways the city can be used by people of all sorts. Walt Whitman once wrote, "All architecture is what you do to it when you look upon it." I would like to broaden that to mean that whatever manufacturers, suppliers, inventors, technicians, professionals, urban planners and designers do in cities must be participated in by many people, must contribute to the growth of the city's life not its death, and must create an environment that people can relate to and feel greater than themselves.

It is this which makes great cities---not architecture nor beautiful ground plans nor green open spaces nor office buildings nor good transportation. Not even full employment nor socially-integrated neighborhoods make a city. It is all of these plus. And the plus is commitment to and enjoyment of a city by diverse and multiple groups of all ages and creative and constantly participatory life of all its citizens.

# UNISONIA

**IMPORTANT INFORMATION I LEARNED IN THIS BOOK**

_____

_____

_____

_____

_____

_____

_____

_____

_____

_____

## CONCLUSIONS

### HUMAN POTENTIAL

New growth opportunities arise for those who are open to accept them. This attitude will be fostered and encouraged through all ages in every method possible, offering administrative assistance, seminars and other services to further human potential, growth and personal success.

UNISONIA does not have a patent on being right and will always be open to evolving ideas, concepts, and suggestions to enrich and fulfill the lives of all UNISONIANS.

### ENVIRONMENTAL LAND USE

Every method which research, experimentation and creative good judgement suggest will be used to make excellent stewardship of the environment and land an attitude to which to aspire. Mutual encouragement and enthusiasm will spread throughout the community.

### COMMUNICATIONS

New communication equipment is constantly being developed to provide updated capability, thereby providing expanded services. Administrative planning services will be practicably networked into the citi-wide communication system.

## ADMINISTRATION

Administration will be constantly open minded to the fulfillment needs of all uni-citizens, striving to make it possible for the community to create a positive, productive environment for all within the community.

## UNISONIA

## WAYS UNISONIA COULD BE IMPROVED UPON

_____

_____

_____

_____

_____

_____

I WILL CONTACT UNISONIA WITH MY SUGGESTIONS

Ivan L. Loesch
Unisonia Institute
PO Box 1374
Huron, SD 57350-1374

# LOESCH

## FRIENDS I SHOULD TALK TO ABOUT UNISONIA

_____

_____

_____

_____

_____

_____

_____

# UNISONIA

## LIST OF ILLUSTRATIONS

## RESOURCES FOR CHANGE
### List of Books and Sources of Information

*The Aquarian Conspiracy,* Marilyn Ferguson, J. P. Tarcher, Inc. 9110 Sunset Blvd., Los Angeles, CA 90096

*MegaTrends,* John Naisbitt, Warner Books, Inc. 75 Rockefeller Plaza, NY., NY 10019

*Community Dreams,* Berkowitz, Impact Publishers PO Box 1094, San Luis Obisbo, CA 93406 - Ph (805)-543-5911

*It Takes A Village,* Hillary Rodham Clinton 319 P $20.00 Simon and Schuster, Rockefeller Center, 1230 Ave of America, NY., NY 10020

*No Place Like Home: Building Sustainable Communities* by Marcia Norzick, Canadian Council on Social Development 55 Parkdale Ave., Ottawa, Ontario K1Y4G1 Phone (613) 728 - 1865; Fax (613) 728-9387

*Creating Community Anywhere: Finding Support and Connection in a Fragmented World,* Carolyn R. Shaffer and Kristan Anundsen, A. Jeremy P. Tarcher/Putnam Book, The Putnam Publishing Group 200 Madison Ave., NY., NY 10016

All of the following materials are available from the Foresight Institute. Please call 913-383-3359 to order.

*Sustainable Cities: Concepts and Strategies for Eco-City Development,* Walter, et.al., 1992, Eco-Home Media, 350 pp., $20.00.

*State of the World Report 1992,* especially chapter on "Shaping Cities," p.119 Lester Brown, et.al., 1992, Worldwatch Institute, 350 pp., $10.95.

*The Death and Life of Great American Cities,* Jane Jacobs, 1961 and 1989, Vintage Books, 450 pp., $12.00.

*Cities and the Wealth of Nations,* Jane Jacobs, 1984, Vintage Books, 350 pp., $6.95.

*The Economies of Cities,* Jane Jacobs, 1969, Vintage Books, 450 pp., $9.00.

*Eco-City Berkeley: Building Cities for a Healthy Future,* Richard Register, 1987, North Atlantic Press, $10.95.

*A Green City Program for San Francisco Bay Cities and Towns,* Peter Berg,et.al., 1990, 82 pp., Planet Drum, Wingbow Press.

*Sustainable Communities: A New Design Synthesis for Cities, Suburbs and Towns,* Van der Ryn & Peter Calthorpe, 1986, Sierra Club, 250 pp., $20.00.

*Co-Housing: A Contemporary Approach to Housing Ourselves,* 1988, Kathryn McCamant and Carles Dujrrett, 1988, 200 pp., Ten Speed Press 550 pp., $42.95. Also, *A Pattern Language and a New Theory of Urban Design.*

*The Integral Urban House,* Olkowski, et.al., 1979, 500 pp., Sierra Club, $7.95.

*The Gaia Atlas of Cities: New Directions in Sustainable Urban Living,* Girardet, Anchor Books/Doubleday, 1992, 191 pp., $16.00.

*End of the Road: The World Car Crisis and How We Can Solve It,* Zuckerman, 1991, Chelsea Green Publishing, 278 pp., $16.95.

*Urban Ecology:* The Journal of Urban Ecology, the only journal devoting itself to the subject at this time reports on progress around the globe.. Individual copies $2, subscription and membership $30, 24 pp

All these resources are available through the Foresight Institute. Please call 913-383-3359 to order.

The *AIA Environmental Resource Guide* (ERG) is a quarterly journal designed to provide architects with resources they need to become more sensitive to environmental concerns.

214

# UNISONIA
## NOTES

# LOESCH

# INFORMATION CHECKOFF

## Please send information on circled items.

| | | | | | | | |
|---|---|---|---|---|---|---|---|
| 1 | 16 | 31 | 46 | 61 | 76 | 91 | 106 |
| 2 | 17 | 32 | 47 | 62 | 77 | 92 | 107 |
| 3 | 18 | 33 | 48 | 63 | 78 | 93 | 108 |
| 4 | 19 | 34 | 49 | 64 | 79 | 94 | 109 |
| 5 | 20 | 35 | 50 | 65 | 80 | 95 | 110 |
| 6 | 21 | 36 | 51 | 66 | 81 | 96 | 111 |
| 7 | 22 | 37 | 52 | 67 | 82 | 97 | 112 |
| 8 | 23 | 38 | 53 | 68 | 83 | 98 | 113 |
| 9 | 24 | 39 | 54 | 69 | 84 | 99 | 114 |
| 10 | 25 | 40 | 55 | 70 | 85 | 100 | 115 |
| 11 | 26 | 41 | 56 | 71 | 86 | 101 | 116 |
| 12 | 27 | 42 | 57 | 72 | 87 | 102 | 117 |
| 13 | 28 | 43 | 58 | 73 | 88 | 103 | 118 |
| 14 | 29 | 44 | 59 | 74 | 89 | 104 | 119 |
| 15 | 30 | 45 | 60 | 75 | 90 | 105 | 120 |

Name: _____

Title: _____

Company: _____

Business Address: _____

City/State/Zip: _____

Telephone: _____

RETURN TO:  Ivan L. Loesch/Unisonia Institute
PO Box 1374, Huron, SD 57350-1374

# LOESCH

I am very interested in making use of every opportunity to be a part of creating a better world for all the earth's inhabitants.

I have checked below my two (2) primary areas of interest in the UNI-CITI plan where I would like to help.

### I. Human Potential

- ☐ Creative human development
- ☐ Health, safety, physical, artistic, mental, music, etc.
- ☐ Spiritual enhancement
- ☐ Educational and mind development

### II. Environmental, Land Use

- ☐ Resource management
- ☐ Effluent, recyclables, solar, transportation
- ☐ Landscapes aesthetics, parks, lakes, lighting, fencing, etc.

### III. Communications

- ☐ Educational, TV, radio, video, print
- ☐ Entertainment, TV, radio, video, print
- ☐ Security and public information - TV, radio, video, paper and scanning

### IV. Administrative Services

- ☐ Administration - financial, personnel
- ☐ Economic development UNI-CENTER, realty, industrial productivity center
- ☐ Planning
- ☐ Human potential, environmental land use, communication

Name: _____ Date: _____

Address:_____

City/State/Zip:_____

Telephone:_____

RETURN TO:   Ivan L. Loesch/Unisonia Institute
PO Box 1374,  Huron, SD 57350-1374

# UNISONIA

## BOOK ORDER CARD

I request _____ additional copies of UNISONIA

@ **$24.95** Per perfect bound copy.

@ **$29.95** Per hard-cover copy.

| | |
|---|---|
| Total for book(s): | $ _____ |
| Shipping/Handling for the first book | $ __5.00__ |
| For each additional book add $3.00: | $ _____ |
| South Dakota tax: .06% | $ _____ |
| Grand total due this order: | $ _____ |

(Institutional Book Orders available at quantity prices)
Allow 4-6 weeks for order processing and delivery.

Please circle form of payment:
    **Money Order**        **MasterCard**        **Visa**

**Credit Card**                              **Exp.**
  **Acct. #:** _____**Date:** _____

**Signature:** _____

**Name:** _____

**Firm:** _____

**Address:** _____

**City/State/Zip:** _____

**Telephone:** _____

**RETURN TO:**   Ivan L. Loesch/Unisonia Institute
                     PO Box 1374,Huron, SD 57350-1374

# LOESCH